Blue Juniata: Collected Poems

Blue Juniata:

Collected Poems

Malcolm Cowley

NEW YORK / THE VIKING PRESS

First published in 1968 by The Viking Press, Inc.
625 Madison Avenue, New York, N.Y. 10022

Published simultaneously in Canada by
The Macmillan Company of Canada Limited

Library of Congress catalog card number: 68-28027

Printed in U.S.A. by The Vail-Ballou Press, Inc.

Among the later poems, "Boy in Sunlight," "The Rocking Chairs,"
"Poverty Hollow," "The Blown Door," "The Pyre," "Passport Blues,"
and "The Living Water" appeared in *Poetry;* "Winter Tenement,"
"Ezra Pound at the Hôtel Jacob," "Voices from Home: 1923," and
"Here with the Long Grass Rippling" appeared in *Saturday Review;*
"Off Campus" in *Harper's;* "Ode in a Time of Crisis" and "The
Enemy Within" in *The Nation;* "The Flower and the Leaf" in *The
Southern Review;* "A Smoke of Birds," "The Silvery Fishes," and "A
Resentment of Rabbits" in *The Roanoke Review;* "Variations on a
Cosmical Air" in *The Sewanee Review;* and "The Chestnut Woods"
in *Between Worlds.* "Stone Horse Shoals," "The End of the World,"
"The Red Branch," and "Piney Woods" appeared originally in *The
New Yorker.* Thanks are due to all these magazines for assignment of
copyright.

"The Time of Crossword Puzzles," first printed in *The Sewanee
Review,* later appeared in *Aragon: Poet of the French Resistance*
(New York: Duell, Sloan & Pearce, Inc., 1945).

To the memory of William and Josephine Cowley

CONTENTS

I: Blue Juniata

Definitions   2
Boy in Sunlight   3
Blue Juniata   5
The Rocking Chairs   6
Dan George   7
Mine No. 6   9
The Hill above the Mine   10
Poverty Hollow   12
Laurel Mountain   13
Overbeck's Barn   15
Processional of the Third Season   19
Day Coach   21
The Blown Door   25
The Chestnut Woods   26
The Pyre   27

II: The Crooked Streets

Note   32
Kelly's Barroom   33
Variations on a Cosmical Air   34
Young Kuppenheimer Gods   36
Nocturne   37
The Rubber Plant   40
Free Clinic   41
Mortality   43
So Perish Time   44
Winter Tenement   46

III: Valuta

Note   48
Valuta   49
Sunrise over the Heiterwand   51
Marizibill   54
Angelica   55
Château de Soupir: 1917   57
Ezra Pound at the Hôtel Jacob   59
The Beach at Palavas   60
Still Life   61
A Smoke of Birds   62
Carnaval in the Midi   63
Two Swans   65
The Peppermint Gardens   66
Voices from Home: 1923   68

IV: The City of Anger

Note   70
Three Songs for Leonora   71
   1. *Circus in Town*   71
   2. *Dumbwaiter Song*   72
   3. *Tennessee Blues*   72
Buy 300 Steel   74
The Eater of Darkness   75
The Flower in the Sea   76
The Narrow House   77
The Turning of the Year   78
Memphis Johnny   79
Tumbling Mustard   81
The Lady from Harlem   82
Restaurateur with Music   83

Commemorative Bronze 84
Those of Lucifer 85
Ten Good Farms 86

V: The Dry Season

Note 88
This Morning Robins 89
The Dry Season 90
The Mother 91
The Firstborn 92
The Long Voyage 93
The Man of Promise 94
Tar Babies 95
Ernest 96
Roxane 97
The Lost People 98
Seven 100

VI: The Unsaved World

Note 102
For St. Bartholomew's Eve (1927) 103
The Last International (1935) 105
Tomorrow Morning (1937) 108
Eight Melons (1937) 110
The End of the World (1940) 111
The Time of Crossword Puzzles (1940–1944) 112
Passport Blues (1947) 114
Ode in a Time of Crisis (1951) 116
The Enemy Within (1952) 117
Here with the Long Grass Rippling (1968) 119

VII: Another Country

Stone Horse Shoals 125

There Is a Moment 127

Leander 128

William Wilson 130

The Living Water 131

Natural History 133

   1. *Piney Woods* 133

   2. *The Silvery Fishes* 133

   3. *A Resentment of Rabbits* 134

   4. *The Red Branch* 134

   5. *The Dog Fox* 135

John Fenstermaker 136

Off Campus 137

The Flower and the Leaf 139

The Urn 142

Index of Titles and First Lines 145

I Blue Juniata

DEFINITIONS

Juniata. A river of west-central Pennsylvania, rising in Somerset County near the crest of the Alleghanies, making its way eastward through deep clefts in several mountain ridges, and falling into the Susquehanna after a tortuous course of about two hundred miles.

Blue Juniata. A sentimental ballad (1844) popular in the middle years of the last century. When I was a boy, very old people in our neighborhood still hummed the tune, but they had forgotten the words except for the first four lines:

> *Wild roved an Indian girl,*
> *Bright Alfarata,*
> *Where sweep the waters*
> *Of the blue Juniata.*

Boy in Sunlight

The boy having fished alone
down Empfield Run from where it started on stony ground,
in oak and chestnut timber,
then crossed the Nicktown Road into a stand
of bare-trunked beeches ghostly white in the noon twi-
    light—

having reached a place of sunlight
that used to be hemlock woods on the slope of a broad
    valley,
the woods cut twenty years ago for tanbark
and then burned over, so the great charred trunks
lay crisscross, wreathed in briars, gray in the sunlight,
black in the shadow of saplings grown
scarcely to fishing-pole size: black birch and yellow birch,
black cherry and fire cherry—

having caught four little trout that float, white bellies up,
in a lard bucket half-full of lukewarm water—
having unwrapped a sweat-damp cloth from a slab of pone
to eat with dewberries picked from the heavy vines—
now sprawls above the brook on a high stone,
his bare scratched knees in the sun, his fishing pole beside
    him,
not sleeping but dozing awake like a snake on the stone.

Waterskaters dance on the pool beneath the stone.
A bullfrog goes silently back to his post among the weeds.
A dragonfly hovers and darts above the water.
The boy does not glance down at them

or up at the hawk now standing still in the pale-blue mountain sky,
and yet he feels them, insect, hawk, and sky,
much as he feels warm sandstone under his back,
or smells the punk-dry hemlock wood,
or hears the secret voice of water trickling under stone.

The land absorbs him into itself,
as he absorbs the land, the ravaged woods, the pale sky,
not to be seen, but as a way of seeing;
not to be judged, but as a way of judgment;
not even to remember, but stamped in the bone.
"Mine," screams the hawk, "Mine," hums the dragonfly,
and "Mine," the boy whispers to the empty land
that folds him in, half-animal, half-grown,
still as the sunlight, still as a hawk in the sky,
still and relaxed and watchful as a trout under the stone.

Blue Juniata

Farmhouses curl like horns of plenty, hide
scrawny bare shanks against a barn, or crouch
empty in the shadow of a mountain. Here
there is no house at all—

only the bones of a house,
lilacs growing beside them,
roses in clumps between them,
honeysuckle over;
a gap for a door, a chimney
mud-chinked, an immense fireplace,
the skeleton of a pine,

and gandy dancers working on the rails
that run not thirty yards from the once door.

I heard a gandy dancer playing on a jew's harp
Where is now that merry party I remember long ago?
Nelly was a lady . . . twice . . . *Old Black Joe,*
as if he laid his right hand on my shoulder,
saying, "Your father lived here long ago,
your father's father built the house, lies buried
under the pine—"
                    Sing *Nelly was a lady*
. . . *Blue Juniata* . . . *Old Black Joe*:

for sometimes a familiar music hammers
like blood against the eardrums, paints a mist
across the eyes, as if the smell of lilacs,
moss roses, and the past became a music
made visible, a monument of air.

The Rocking Chairs

At seven o'clock, when tables had been cleared,
their oilcloth tops wiped clean, and children sent
outdoors for hide-and-seek, and chairs put straight,
and dishes scraped and washed and put away—
at seven o'clock the village wives appeared
on the front porches, all took spindle-backed
high rocking chairs and swayed in unison,
smartly at first, as slippers tapped, one, two,
then lingeringly, one and . . . two and . . . one.

At eight o'clock, "The house was hot," one says,
and Mabel says, "The house was hot today,
and not a cloud in the sky, but a stormy moon
last night with the horns turned down, so maybe rain
will come by morning." July, the windless month,
when dust in the road is barefoot deep, when children
count in a circle, sibbety, sab, kanawba,
then run away to hide from rocking chairs
on porches creaking, one . . . and two . . . and one.

At nine o'clock a streetlong sound of doors
banged shut and latched against the stranger. Soon
in every house a yellowness of lamps,
and nobody left watching in the darkness
—except one boy, his playmates gone to bed,
who heard night insects creak like rocking chairs,
who saw lamps carried, shadows cross the wall
of rooms now barred to him, and saw the mothers
stiff-backed in gingham climb the secret stairs.

Dan George

He chews tobacco, tips the dusty brim
of a black felt hat and says,
                    "I was top sergeant,
they killed the captain and the two lieutenants,
for eight months the company was mine."
Sergeant Dan George, wounded at Chickamauga,
    prisoner at Andersonville.

Dignity is an old man dribbling tobacco juice
on the yellow ends of his cavalry mustache.

"Listen, Dan George"—your skin is china brown,
your eyes gone pale, your fingers gentle and long
as those of the mist—"you ran away to fight,
came home to drink with the wild paddy boys,
drove a hard bargain with your neighbors, stole
their virgin timberland, slept with their wives?"

"Maybe." He smiled down at the dust. "I don't
rightly remember. A long time ago."

I used to find him in the Presbyterian
graveyard, limping among the stiff blue cedars,
spelling over a tomb:
                    "Humpty Mert Miller,
ran a water sawmill in Pine Flats,
a hard man, a good hater, died fighting drunk.
Bury me at his side—"
                    and three words more,

remembered from a song—"where woodbine twineth,"
looking at woodbine tangled on a grave.

Now Reverend Death, when he comes driving through
Pine Township in his black three-seated rig,
whoaing the horses, calling from a gate,
"Jump in, Eliza!—Cain, there's room, jump in!"
(nobody calls back to him) —
                            when Death
in his black suit and celluloid collar turns
into Dan George's lane, nobody speaks,
nobody stirs but the old man chewing tobacco,
thinking of Chickamauga and his friends.

Dan George climbed into the surrey, took the reins,

and somewhere was a noise of lamentation,
grief without pain, an unembittered moan,
old lonesome women weeping in every farmhouse
on the road from Pine Flats to Cherry Tree.

Mine No. 6

They scoured the hill with steel and living brooms
of fire, that none else living might persist;
here crouch their cabins, here the tipple looms
uncompromising, black against the mist.

All day their wagons lumber past, the wide
squat wheels hub deep, the horses strained and still;
a headlong rain pours down all day to hide
the blackened stumps, the ulcerated hill.

Beauty, perfection, I have loved you fiercely
—even in this windy slum, where fear
drips from the eaves with April rain, and scarcely
a leaf sprouts, and a wilderness in pain
brings forth its monstrous children—even here
. . . your long white cruel fingers at my brain.

The Hill above the Mine

Nobody comes to the graveyard on the hill,
sprawled on the ash-gray slope above the mine,
where coke-oven fumes drift heavily by day
and creeping fires at night. Nobody stirs
here by the crumbled wall where headstones loom
among the blackberry vines. Nobody walks
in the blue starlight under cedar branches,
twisted and black against the moon, or speaks
except the mustered company of the dead,

and one who calls the roll.
                              "Ezekiel Cowley?"
Dead.
          "Laban and Uriah Evans?"
                                      Dead.
"Jasper McCullough, your three wives, your thirty
acknowledged children?"
                          Dead to the last child,
most of them buried here on the hillside, hidden
under the brambles, waiting with the others
above the unpainted cabins and the mine.

What have you seen, O dead?
                              "We saw our woods
butchered, flames curling in the maple tops,
white ashes drifting, a railroad in the valley
bridging the creek, and mine shafts under the hill.
We saw our farms lie fallow and houses grow
all summer in the flowerless meadows. Rats

all winter gnawed the last husks in the barn.
In spring the waters rose, crept through the fields
and stripped them bare of soil, while on the hill
we waited and slept firm."

Wait on, O dead!

The waters still shall rise, the hills fold in,
the graves open to heaven, and you shall ride
eastward on a rain wind, wrapped in thunder,
your white bones drifting like herons across the moon.

Poverty Hollow

Here in a mountain valley
we worked our fields till even the bottom land
was ribbed and gaunt as the horses, as the men.
This year our corn is blighted.
The valley is too narrow, and we have driven
our plows against the bony shanks of a hill.

Now rest, my brothers,
lie down together in a furrow. Rest,
and some day when the mineral earth has grown
cold as the moon's craters, when the sun
fades in perpetual starlight, then our hills
will fold like wrinkles in a forehead, press
the valley out between them like slow fingers
against a bone-hard thumb, and so provide
for us magnificent burial, my kin.

Cold hills already lie
staring down at our cornfields hungrily.

Laurel Mountain

Listen: we were working in the woods
on Laurel Mountain somewhere, and the rain
against our roof that rusted, a windless rain
dripped all night in the tangles of our hair.

All night the trickle of rain across our faces,
the hiss of raindrops on a sheet-iron stove
until the fire went dead. In the gray morning
three men together left the shack and tramped

into the hemlock woods that smelled of rain.
Three twisted men together in the woods,
two of them sawing a hemlock tree, and one
who faced them chopping, till the ax-head broke,

split from the wet helve, and one man fell.
Grunting he fell on his knees in the cold moss,
wiped blood away from his eyes, cursed God, and died.
Reuben and Simeon: we were his two sons,

his tall sons twisted with their anger, cold
with hatred for his body. Spring was late.
Corn froze that year in June. The woods were bare.
We hollowed out a grave in the wet woods,

laid him among the hemlock roots face down,
and fetched a spray of dogwood for his hair,
I don't know why, then shoveled the dirt in,
tramping it firm with muddy boots. The rain

beat steadily on our shoulders hunched in prayer
against a tall God like a hemlock tree,
his arms like crooked branches, his head bare,
his voice a cold rain dripping in the moss,
and hemlock needles tangled in his hair.

Overbeck's Barn

In our country the barns are built four-square,
with doors for high-stacked wagonloads of wheat
and diamonds cut high up on the gable ends
   to let the swallows in.
We used to say that Overbeck's barn floor
was clean enough to eat your dinner off it,
if Overbeck would feed you. A hard man
he was to neighbors, but gentle to the land
and proud of what it yielded. "Empty barn,
   dead farm," he used to say.

The last week in July they threshed his wheat
behind the barn. Upstairs in the pink bedroom,
in the four-post bed, under the flowered quilt,
old Simon Overbeck lay dying. "Move
my bed to the window. Put another pillow
under my head. Raise higher. Leave me now,
Annie and all the rest. I feel dead tired.
   I want to see the farm."

The square bulk of the barn hid most of it.

He heard the roar of sheaves in the separator,
when belts ran slack, the chut-chut of the tractor,
but only saw the jutting pipe of the stacker
and straw that poured in a river from its tip:
   straw in a waterfall,
   chaff in a yellow mist.
He said to himself, "Tell Walter to watch the hands,
most of them lazy, and all those mouths to feed."

His eyes were rheumy. He wiped them with the sheet,
then saw a stubble field beyond the barn,
farther the green of month-old buckwheat, farther
his woods that ended in a shadowy line.
They touched the house almost, there were no fields,
the time he came here first in a new wagon,
proud of his new wife, fifty years ago.

    She dressed in printed cotton.
    They owned a stumpy clearing
    in the pine woods, a cabin
    empty and windowless, no barn.
Leaving the horses hitched to a chestnut root,
he took a double handful of black loam,
sifted it slowly through his fingers, fetched
his ax from under the wagon seat, and chopped
    the tallest of the pines.

He was a hard man, Simon, hard to himself,
working into the dusk to clear his fields,
then watching the piled logs that burned all night,
hard to his neighbors too. They raised his barn
one spring and got no thanks. He never loaned them
a plugged nickel, but he bought their land
in hungry seasons, if the price was right
(forty acres, once, for a span of mules,
harness thrown in). That was his valley field.
Next spring he'd plant his corn there, but seed down
the slopes in clover to keep the soil from washing.

"Buy hogs to fatten. Pork is due for a rise,"
he said to himself, while knowing that the hogs,
bought or unbought, would thrive or sicken, corn
would rustle as it grew in the August night,
    and he not there to listen.

"Walter will have it all.
  Walter is flighty.
He'll tear up everything to suit hisself
  and finish nothing.
Walter is bone lazy like the hands.
  The farm will go to sticks."

He looked at the fields and knew that he was wrong.

"Walter is like the other Overbecks.
  They settle down.
The farm is stronger than all the Overbecks.
The farm will keep on growing and me dead."

  He heard the dinner bell.
  The tractor grumbled a moment.
  The belt slapped and was still.
Now there were voices. Under them he heard
the enormous insect creaking of the fields,
not his fields any longer. He was seized
with sudden furious longing to destroy
present and past, to let the cattle starve
tied in their stalls, to mow the buckwheat green,
chop down the woods, poison the well, plant corn
on the steepest hillside, so the summer rains
would scour it down to rock, and so the farm
that he created with his living hands
might die with him by flood—by fire? The barn?
"Oh, merciful Christ," he prayed for the first time,
  "give me the strength to rise.
  There's matches on the dresser.
  The straw is dry as a bone."

He strained upward. He clenched his chalky hands
as if they held the farm. His face went white.

His head fell back on the pillow,
which Annie had embroidered with an O
in purple cotton, and she brought it out
for special occasions only. People said
she was a grand good housewife, Simon was
a hard man who never prayed nor helped
a soul in trouble, but only loved his land.
The way he was taken off it was a judgment.

Processional of the Third Season

The year declines now formally to his end
(cover him over, scatter the dead leaves over)'.
Countrymen, neighbors, let us take the body
and hollow out a place and bury him
   (plows and harrows and sixty horses) .

We Strongstown men together can bear an arm
of him, Mahaffey's Mills can bear another,
and Nicktown and Pine Flats each having taken
a leg of him, our villages will march
westward across the fields with the dead year
   (cover him over) .

   Plows and harrows and sixty horses
will make a path for him and all that follows:
turkeys in flocks, white geese, a fattened steer
convoyed by girls, the aproned women riding
in wagons heaped with sides of bacon, hams,
the first and whitest flour, the yellowest meal,
the headiest cider. Let his wake be merry,
and while the sunlight fades on Chestnut Ridge,
   scatter the dead leaves over.

Hollow a place for his head by the Dunkard church
   (plows and harrows and sixty horses) ;
lay his feet by the meeting house at Bethel;
furrow his limbs ten inches deep in loam
from field to level field across the township.
Now we shall kill and roast the ox, now spit

the geese and turkeys, broach the casks of cider,
eat hugely and love deep. Over his grave
the young wheat will prosper in the spring.

Cover him over. Scatter the dead leaves over.

Day Coach

1

Tickets please tickets.
He settled back, please tickets, in the seat
and let himself go numb to the fingertips,
his mind in animal reverie, kept warm
by remembered things as by an overcoat.

Climbing an apple tree behind the barn . . .
tickets please, ticketsplease, ticketsplease, tickets.
The click of the wheels rose to a higher clack.
Strangers came lurching down the aisle and touched
only the frayed coattails of his dream.

Miles afterward he roused to watch the hills
weave up and down like green ungraceful dancers
projected on the curtain of his eyes,
while houses fled in a rabble, and his breath
took shape in clouds that wavered on the pane.

2

As the Limited swept past them, he found himself looking into a woman's eyes with momentary perfect compre-
hension. Through the plate glass of the dining car—the
other—he saw a fork suspended in air, and before it had
changed position he was staring into a smoking car where
four men played cards on a suitcase clamped to their knees.
The other brakeman vanished as he smiled. Here was a city
tucked into a special-delivery envelope and sealed with the
red taillight how stately in its progress up the track. A

world sealed out of his own world and living for fifty seconds of his life.

3

"The bell that suddenly greets us at a crossing
and dies as suddenly—somewhere the bell
 rings on for other trains.

"A woman at an open door stands waving
a handkerchief to all of us. Three boys
come racing down a hill to see us pass.
A man fishes in a muddy river.

"He disappears. Somewhere the handkerchief
still waves and children race to meet a train,
and I, if I descended from the train,
might end my days in one of these brief towns
that overhang a momentary river."

4

The lights of the train now move
transversely across the water;
across the water strides
the shadow of the engineer;
barred rows of window shine across the water
as if they marked a prison that exists
nowhere on solid earth, but always bears
us the condemned across a world of water.

5

Time is recorded not by minutes, but by station stops;
we are two stops east of Altoona, one stop west of it;
Cresson, Cres-son, change cars for Luckett, Munster, and all

points on the line that runs crookedly back into a boyhood,
with the burden of an hour dropping like October fruit at
every revolution of the driving wheel and a year lost at
each of the grimy remembered stations: Ebensburg, Beulah
Road, Nant-y-glo. Gather your luggage and move it to the
door. Twin Rocks.

6

"O travelers, with you
I moved like a firefly over twilight waters;
    with you I was spit
like a cherry stone from the puckered lips of the tunnel,
then blindly plunged with you into seas of light.

"Travelers all!
            Let us join hands and dance
to very old music, *Farmer in the dell*
and *London Bridge is falling down*, once, twice,
around our faithful locomotive.
                        Come!

"Those others, will they join us from their cabs
and tenders, from the roundhouse, from the tower,
or from the red caboose that sleeps behind
a string of empty freight cars, where a lantern
gathers the whole of night in one pale flame?"

7

Out of the group that lingered at the station
no single form detached itself to meet him.
The circle of their backs was a wall against him.

Oblongs of light reflected from the train
gleamed for a moment on the mountainside.
A whistle drifted eastward with the wind.

He buttoned his coat and walked into the darkness,
which step by step preceded him, until
he stopped as if to rest it on his shoulders.

Feeling the weight of darkness on his shoulders,
he stumbled on with his burden of trees and hills.

The Blown Door

I watched for years a sidehill farm that died
   a little, day by day.
Branch after branch the dooryard maples died
and a buckwheat field was gullied into clay,

to the beat . . . beat of a loose board on the barn
   that flapped in the wind all night;
nobody came to drive a nail in it.
The farm died in a broken window light,

a broken pane upstairs in the east bedroom
   that let the northeast rain
beat down all night on the red Turkey carpet;
nobody puttied in another pane.

Nobody nailed a new slat on the corncrib;
   nobody mowed the hay
or swung a gate that sagged on rusty hinges.
The farm died when two boys went away,

or lived until the lame old man was buried.
   I came then, and once more
to see how sumac overspread the pasture,
to smell dead leaves and hear a gust of wind
somewhere inside the house blow shut a door.

The Chestnut Woods

While nobody's million eyes are blinking, come!

    It is too late now.

Come far, and find a place where orchard grass,
blue grass and fescue, white and yellow clover
tangle an orchard slope, and juneberries
ripen and fall at the edge of the deep woods.

    Highways and areaways,
    eyes, numbers, unremembered days;
    it is too late now.

Since unremembered days the ferns have grown
knee deep, and moss under the chestnut trees
hiding the footprints of small deer. You ran
and I ran after, till we reached the spring
that flows from underneath the chestnut roots
in a bright stream, we traced it through the laurel,
crossing burned ground where briars clawed us back,
then headlong crashing down a hill to find—

    and lose again and now it is too late.
    We have lived a long time under sheet-iron skies
    in neon-haggard dreams where no moons rise;
    the juneberries will be withered on the branches;
    the chestnut woods are dead.

The Pyre

Strangers were buying the house,
"Our summer home," his mother called it,
but always it was their real home.
Now everything in it had to be sold—

the barrels and trunks in the attic,
the stone crocks in the cellar,
the treasures in his mother's china closet
and the closet too, with one cracked side;
the bearskin rug with big jaws that scared his little sister,
the blackberry preserve that his mother had ranged in jars
      on the pantry shelves,
and the bed where she died.

Everything had to be sold,
but it wouldn't be fair to take the first offer;
that wouldn't be playing the game.
"Yes, Mrs. Powers, I was born in this room.
I had my first bath in that big china washbowl
there, with the blue flowers.
No, I don't think a quarter would be enough.
Fifty cents, with all the memories thrown in
and a cake of soap, Mrs. Powers."

Everything had to be sold at a fair price.
It was his duty to joke and wheedle,
to say, "Mrs. Altemus, I know you want only the best,"
or even, to Milt Bracken who was ailing,
and the beds were hard to sell,
"That was my mother's bed, with two good mattresses,
Milt, you can sleep there well."

It was what they expected,
and they were his own hard-worked, hard-minded people,
shapes of his childhood, patterns of his growth.
He would play the part they wanted him to play,
while feeling it was sin and penance both,
torture and solace both.

And still,
one thing he would not sell:
a little dropleaf desk in the upstairs hall
that belonged to his sister Ruth, dead long ago
when he was away at school.
Here in the desk he found her pencil box,
a doll with one squint eye and frizzly hair,
a set of building blocks,
and a red satin ribbon, the last she wore:
tokens of Ruth that his mother had saved.
It was no use saving them any more.

Two girls in pigtails came giggling up the stairs.
He didn't know their names,
but one of them was nine, Ruth's age, and he gave her the
    desk,
then gave the building blocks to her little sister.
Everything else he carried into the yard
and burned, even the frizzly-headed doll,
on a pyre of twenty-year-old newspapers.

The pale flames turned red.
He heard Milt Bracken shouting to his sons
as two of them carried out the bed.

"Ruth," he said, "Ruth,
you have died three times,
once in the flesh, once when your mother died,

and now again with your last treasures.
The black-haired squalling baby I detested,
the child I was sent to wheel in her gocart,
walking behind it shamefaced, yet in pride,
the schoolgirl racing home
to her blocks and her books and her doll with a squint eye—
all these and my own boyhood,
the big frame house under the locust tree,
the land itself, the woods in chestnut season,
the spring plowing, the hayfields in July—
all these and your mother's grief
consumed with the pencil box and the satin hair ribbon,
drifting in smoke into the pale sky."

II The Crooked Streets

NOTE

After college, after the war, some of us drifted to New York, to the crooked streets south of Fourteenth, where one could rent a gaslit hall bedroom for three dollars a week or the top floor of a rickety house for thirty dollars a month. There were two schools among us: those who painted the floors black (they were the last of the aesthetes) and those who did not paint them. Our college textbooks and the complete works of Jules Laforgue gathered dust on the mantelpiece among a litter of unemptied ashtrays. The streets outside were those of Glenn Coleman's early paintings: low red-brick early-nineteenth-century houses, crazy doorways, sidewalks covered with black snow, and, in the foreground, an old woman bending under a sack of rags.

In that setting of grime and poverty we spent the postwar years, scantily clothed, poorly fed, signing drafts against our abundant constitutions, and greatly enjoying ourselves. There was much in our surroundings that agreed with our mood. Having lost our illusions proudly, at an early age, we felt the need of replacing them with others, and we had made a kind of religion out of the sordid. We worshiped the cluttered streets, the overflowing ash barrels, the houses full of people and rats; we felt something like veneration for the barrooms then in their last months of legal existence; and our writings, besides a self-protective smirk, had the smell of sawdust, youth, squalor, and Luke O'Connor's beer-and-stout.

Kelly's Barroom

Always I felt a love for sordid things,
alleys and courtyards, airless tragedies,
whispers in closets, poverty, amours
in the live darkness, swift and sinister.

These gangs parading, drunken, pale, these girls
who meet their kind like cats in areaways,
these cluttered streets of theirs, and filthy rooms,
and death around the corner I have found
voluptuous.

The crowd is here tonight;
the nickel-in-the-slot piano plays
Oh, take me back, please take me back to—where
do broken-voiced pianos hope to go?
A floozie sobs tonight, "I'm lonely, please,
Arthur, give me a drink, I'm awful lonely,"
and Arthur humming as he mops the bar.

Tonight I too am lonely for the soil:
Oh, take me back, please take me back—to home,
innocence, the family, marriage, these
ancestral dreams, these melodies of the race.

Variations on a Cosmical Air

Love is the flower of a day,
love is a rosebud—anyway,
when we propound its every feature,
we make it sound like horticulture,
and even in our puberty
we drown love in philosophy.

> *But I'm coming around in a taxi, honey,*
> *tomorrow night with a roll of money.*
> *You wanna be ready 'bout ha-past eight.*

As celibates we cerebrate
tonight, we stutter and perplex
our minds with Death and Time and Sex;
we dream of star-sent, heaven-bent
plans for perpetual betterment;
tomorrow morning we shall curse
to find the self-same universe.

> *Frankie and Johnny were lovers—*
> *Lordy, how those two could love!*
> *They swore to be true to each other,*
> *just as true as the stars above.*

The stars above my attic chamber
are old acquaintances of mine
and closer now than I remember;
the moon, a last year's valentine,
coquets with me, though growing fusty;
the Milky Way is pale and dusty.

"Freud is my shepherd, there are no sins,"
whispers the Virgin to the Twins.

Even the best of friends must part;
put your money on the dresser before you start.

Before I start let planets break
and suns turn black before I wake
alone tomorrow in this room;
I want a cosmic sort of broom
to reach the Bear and Sirius even,
annihilate our ancient heaven,
or rearrange in other pairs
those interstellar love affairs,
finding a mate for everyone
and me, and me, before I'm done.

Ashes to ashes and dust to dust,
stars for love and love for money;
if the whisky don't get you the cocaine must,
and I'm coming around in a taxi, honey.

Young Kuppenheimer Gods

Linda the manicurist, close beside
her lover-boy, a junior in the Street,
clings to his arm and whispers, while the tide
comes sedulously licking at their feet,

then creeps away. She sends her glances roving
among the bathers, judging every feature.
This is a place, she thinks, for pleasant loving,
no more than comfortably close to nature

and rich in social graces. Marching by
are Kuppenheimer gods in bathing suits,
upholstered queens, and flappers bare of thigh.
Sand filters into patent-leather boots.

The sun beats down on painted cheeks. The sea
nags at the littered beach complainingly.

Nocturne

Ces enfants, à quoi rêvent-elles,
Dans les ennuis des ritournelles?
—LAFORGUE

Mother has washed the dishes, limped upstairs;
Mother has disappeared into the light;
porches are filled where wicker rocking chairs
creak . . . through the emptiness of night
. . . creak . . . scrape, as if they would repeat
the litany of the daughters of this street:

> *"Hamburg steak for supper, ladders in our hose,*
> *nobody speaks of them, everybody knows;*
> *meeting me at twilight, he handed me a rose:*
> *will he come?*

"Will he come with gallant eyebrows, chestnut hair;
will he come and rock beside me in the chair;
will he press my fingers neatly, say discreetly,
life is real,
life is true, will he tell its every secret,
but discreetly,
having realized how sacredly I feel?"

Let me tiptoe through the darkness, boldly whisper,
"He will come;
he will come and take your hand,
swiftly choosing you for queen;
he will take you to the wedding in his limousine;
he will tell you life is true, and understand
what only you and he can understand."

Through the night her sticky hand
reaches out and touches mine.
"It is you that understand,
it must be you."

"No, I'm sorry."
                    "But it's true,
true . . . that you beside me in the chair
will tell me all of life and how to play,
will ask me for my hand—"
                              I shall say
. . . what shall I say?

"Your folk are stronger than mine,
    being less bold;
your arms are stronger than mine,
    willing to hold;
your faith is stronger than mine,
    founded on lies;
my faith is no longer mine,
but melts away in your eyes,
in the syrup of your eyes.
I can never belong to you."

And she: "It is not true."

My words have tapped like pebbles
in the dry well of her mind.
She only smiles and echoes,
"It is not true. You are unkind,"
or else she answers nothing of the kind.

She will say nothing, and I . . . nothing,
only to kiss her fingers, slip away
past willow rockers creaking in the darkness;
if willow chairs could speak, these would say:

> *"He will come, don't despair,*
> *oval smiles and chestnut hair:*
> *he will come."*

The Rubber Plant

Can you see their angular shadows on the blind?

If ever the rubber plant
ceased to project the crossbars of its leaves
against the cord portières;
if the gilt clock no longer
spied down on them from the mantelpiece,
and folding doors were suddenly thrown open,
they could take hands and stride out regally
into—

    Yes, that is it exactly,
at least it is possible.

Free Clinic

1

Rows of soiled faces parallel
the benches, which in turn
parallel the reception desk,
run perpendicular to the drug
counter, and are bisected by
an aisle that stops
                    at a given
point.

In another world are tangents, arcs,
chords, ovals . . . but the aisle,
which parallels the wall, bisects
the room and at a given point
stops.

2

Mrs. Magrady,
gray hat, gray dress, gray
dirty quivering flesh:
she is dumped on the seat
like a barrel of ashes.
                    What
ever can be the matter with you
today, Mrs. Magrady?

3

God is an old woman
with dropsy—

　　　　　　or perhaps
you were not created
in His image?

　　　　4

About the progress of a fly
up these funereal walls there is a
something.
　　　　　　(One remembers
Caesar marching through a burned city
alone.)

　　　　5

In a circle of perfume
two shopgirls, one with a rose
stuck in a ragged buttonhole, and one
with a petaled sore.
　　　　　　　　"It ain't my fault,
honest, Doctor."

　　　　6

Against a colorless skin the brazen
　　loveliness of a tumor,
fistula, chancre, chancroid—
　　it is not
because I admired their beauty,
　　no, tormented
by the search for the white absolute,
by the nostalgia of the immaculate
conception . . . I therefore

Mortality

Death is an accumulation of infirmities: hairs fall, a tooth
decays, and death; a spot of eczema returns each year
with spring; death hides itself in a pimple, a bruise,
a sty,

or lurks beside the lips in a parenthesis that deepens no
longer; death is rigid, being the achievement of a pattern; death is a finished pattern of wrinkles round the
eye.

Having completed some grand work, to die. . . .

Considered abstractly, death is a process of exteriorization;
the possible is realized and buried; thought builds a
mausoleum for itself; the brain is engraved in granite
or a lie.

An apple at bedtime; coffee at nine each morning with two
lumps, please, and heavy cream at nine; death is the
growth of habits, and we die

at the top first; toes are the last to turn toward the daisies,

eyes having first looked sightless at the sky.

So Perish Time

Nothing lives here, he says in the darkening room,
except a clock that ticks its heart away
brassily on a nickel-plated breast.
Everything else is dead that lived by day,
and dust seeps down on the worn bedspread, dust
sifts in through torn lace curtains, making queer
gratings of sunset, like the bars of a tomb.
Be very quiet, the dead are sleeping here.

    Twilight. And still the clock
    ticks brassily at every second.
    The minutes stalk
    grimly across the field of consciousness.
    An hour is time unreckoned.
    Precise and categorical,
    the seconds hammer on the wall.

At their touch the flesh disintegrates;
the mind is reduced to cerebrum and cerebellum,
in grayish whorls like a ball of cotton waste,
a bundle of soiled linen, a bale of shoddy.
The seconds drip from a great height,
exploding one by one against his nerves,
against the broken carapace of body.
Each second is eroding like the rain
its bit of flesh or deliquescent brain.

    So perish tyranny! said the philosopher, taking his
    alarm clock and tossing it into the hall. So perish time!
    The clock rolled downstairs, punctuating his remarks
    with a bump on each step, as if it were proclaiming that

rhythm is the essence of life, life, can I find it, life, said
the philosopher and then

went back to his accustomed place.
The room had grown so dark he could not see,
leaving him out of time and space,
whirled in an eddy of infinity;
and yet his heart beat seventy beats to the minute;
time was drumming at the taut skin of his temples;
time dripped through his veins.

Winter Tenement

When everything but love was spent
we climbed five flights above the street
and wintered in a tenement.
It had no bathroom and no heat
except a coal fire in the grate
that we kept burning night and day
until the fire went out in May.

There in a morning ritual,
clasping our chilblained hands, we joked
about the cobwebs on the wall,
the toilet in the public hall,
   the fire that always smoked.
We shivered as we breakfasted,
then to get warm went back to bed.

In the black snows of February
that rickety bed an arm's-length wide
became our daylong sanctuary,
our Garden of Eden, till we spied
one spring morning at our bedside,
   resting on his dull sword,
the rancorous angel of the bored.

"We raised this cockroach shrine to love,"
I said; "here let his coffin lie.
Get up, put coffee on the stove
to drink in memory of love,
then take the uptown train, while I
sit here alone to speculate
and poke the ashes in the grate."

III Valuta

NOTE

In the years from 1920 to 1924 old Europe, that continent of hierarchies and values, had ceased to have any values whatever; it had only prices, which changed from country to country, from village to village, and especially from day to day. I remember banquets in Germany for which the bill amounted to a nickel (or was it eight cents?) and packs of cigarettes that I bought for the price of a week's lodging.

Those new conditions produced a new race of tourists, the *Valutaschweine*, the profiteers of the exchange, who wandered from France to Rumania, from Italy to Poland, in search of the vilest prices and the most picturesque upheavals of society. Indifferent to the past of Europe, they were seen more often in night clubs than in museums or cathedrals; but especially they could be seen in the railroad station at Innsbruck: Danes, Hindus, Yankees, South Americans, wine-cheeked Englishmen, and still more Yankees, all of them waiting for the international express that would bear them toward the rapidly falling Reichsmark or the unstabilized lira.

Among those pilgrims of the pound sterling and the dollar were younger people who regarded themselves as pilgrims of art. Indifferent as the others to what Europe had been, they moved, as one of them said, "amid the most admired disorder." And many of them wrote poems from day to day, sometimes in a great chilly hotel room in Tyrol, sometimes in a French pension near the Mediterranean, and sometimes in Berlin, crouching beside a porcelain stove and scarcely hearing the roars outside that came, perhaps, from a mob.

Valuta

Following the dollar, ah, following the dollar, I learned
   three fashions of eating with the knife and ordered
   beer in four languages from a Hungarian waiter while
   following the dollar eastward along the forty-eighth
   parallel of north latitude—where it buys most, there is
   the Fatherland—

following the dollar by gray Channel seas, by blue seas in
   Italy, by Alpine lakes as blue as aniline blue, by lakes
   as green as a bottle of green ink, with ink-stained mountains rising on either hand,

I dipped my finger in the lake and wrote, *I shall never return, never, to my strange land:*

my land where plains are daily stretched, where forests burn
   in business hours daily, where yellow nameless rivers
   run, and where

cities stand daily on their heads to raise proud legs in the
   air;

my land of cowboys, of businessmen, of peddlers peddling
   appliances to boil an egg three minutes, exactly three
   minutes, and one born every minute in my land

incomprehensible and sweet and far, where bold Doug Fair-
   banks weds our winsome Mary, and taking the Bronx
   Express they sail away, far, far away, into a photo-
   graphed bliss I never shall understand.

Four angels glory-haunted guard my land:

at the north gate Theodore Roosevelt, at the south gate
    Jack Johnson, at the west gate Charlie Chaplin, and

at the middle gate a back-country fiddler from Clarion
    County fiddling, with a turkey in the straw and a haw,
    haw, haw, and a turkey in the hay and I shall never
    hear it fiddled, ah, farther than Atlantis is my land,

where I could return tomorrow if I chose,

but I shall return to it never;

shall never wed my pale Alaska virgin;

in thine arms lie nevermore, ah, Texas Rose.

Sunrise over the Heiterwand

The house was full of light,
so full of light it bulged at every window,
and when he opened the door,
what was the music rippling down the pathway,
what laughter that pursued him through the gate?

The enchanted smile of Circe has lost its cunning.

Oh, to escape from these dominical
vulgarities, the laughter of the harpy
in my pursuit, the phonograph that plays
Weine nicht, Liebchen and *That Swanee Shore*:
climb, climb the mountain into another air.

He left the siren's house at nightfall, climbed
all night, skirting the brink of precipices
(the fog hid them) and leaping the crevasse.
The vegetation changed as he rose higher,

poplars giving place to beeches,
beeches giving place to larches,
larches giving place to meadows,
meadows blanching into snow.
Climb farther, climb.

Above the last sparse meadows among the snow
there hides the flower I chose for my device,
excelsior, among the snowdrifts hidden,
in snowdrifts blooming and fading, edelweiss.

I plucked an edelweiss;
I held the flower proudly to my lips,
standing alone on the highest precipice,
baying aloud to the moon.
Suddenly I found her at my side.

The moon took refuge under the Heiterwand.

Whose was the moment of grim ecstasy
among the snows, when over the Heiterwand
burst forth the crimson unexpected sun?
And whose the blood that stained the snow at dawn?

White. No word spoken. A thunder in the dawn.

She was gone suddenly, floating into space.
The gulf was bottomless. I leaped to follow.

And silently as feathers do, he fell,
he floated down past layer after layer
of vegetation, larches, beeches, poplars,
then farther down,
descending faster and faster, he sees the palm,
the baobab, the banyan heavy with creepers
and creeping beasts over the dead lagoon.

It was beside the dead lagoon he died.

The angel horde takes flight: what hands are lifting him,
    and who has seized the four bruised members, and who
    has taken the head?

They are swinging him ever upward and they are singing
    hymns to his praise in honor of the dead.

They are singing angel hymns in ancient Hebrew: he sings
their hymns in Hebrew as he rises, *me'erez*, out of the
land of Egypt rising, *mizraim*, out of the house of bond-
age rising to sing, and rises ever

into that rarer ether which is breathed by mortal lips, by
mortal lungs, ah, never.

Marizibill

After the French of Apollinaire

In the High Street of Cologne
evenings she used to come and pass,
crying herself to who would own,
then swollen-footed she would sit
and drink in evil bars alone.

Her trinkets were in pawn to buy
clothes for a pimp with orange hair,
a garlicky smell, a Tartar eye,
who coming from Macao had found
her in a brothel in Shanghai.

People I've known of every sort—
unequal to their destinies
they hover in the wind like spores;
their eyes are not-quite-smothered fires;
their hearts hang open like their doors.

Angelica

Translucent fingers on the yellow keys,
the shadow of a smile upon her lips,
Angélique plays. "Lovely, those rhapsodies,"
we say, drinking our tea in noiseless sips.
   "What tone she has, what soul!
How she must work, and how her hands are clever!"
Although you still embroider for your hope chest,
Angelica, and though your fragrant hair
is soft as lilacs beside you in a bowl,
   they will never marry you, never.

In the gilt mirror, the corners of your eyes,
   see, they already are
drawn in too-fragile patterns like your laces.
   The young men died in the war.

   Lamenting them forever,
your hands will forever drone across the keys
like wind among the bamboos, harmonies
heard dimly like a tinkle of distant cowbells.
   It ceases never;
the last chord will never be resolved,
but always it will hang in dusty corners
behind closed doors that nevermore swing back.
Empty the house will be of guests and mourners;
only yourself among the bric-a-brac,

only yourself to live among the echoes,
to watch the web of delicate lines that spread
from day to day, encroaching on your smile,
to watch the lilac nimbus leave your head,

and fingers yellowing like ivories,
and they will set you on the mantelpiece
to keep a faithful watch over your dead.

Beside a bowl of artificial fruit,
beside a clock that never strikes the hours,
or maybe strikes in other centuries,
you will be set upon the mantelpiece,
a flower in a wax bouquet of flowers.

Château de Soupir: 1917

Jean tells me that the Senator
came here to see his mistresses.
With a commotion at the door
the servants ushered him, Jean says,
through velvets and mahoganies
to where the odalisque was set,
the queen pro tempore, Yvette.

An eighteenth-century château
remodeled to his Lydian taste,
painted and gilt fortissimo:
the Germans, grown sardonical,
had used a bust of Cicero
as shield for a machine-gun nest
at one end of the banquet hall.

The trenches run diagonally
across the gardens and the lawns,
and jagged wire from tree to tree.
The lake is desolate of swans.
In tortured immobility
the deities of stone or bronze
abide each new catastrophe.

Phantasmagorical at nights,
yellow and white and amethyst,
the star-shells flare, the Verey lights
hiss upward, brighten, and persist
until a tidal wave of mist
rolls over us and makes us seem
the drowned creatures of a dream,

ghosts among earlier ghosts. Yvette,
the tight skirt raised above her knees,
beckons her lover *en fillette,*
then nymphlike flits among the trees,
while he, beard streaming in the breeze,
pants after her, a portly satyr,
his goat feet shod in patent leather.

The mist creeps riverward. A fox
barks underneath a blasted tree.
An enemy machine gun mocks
this ante-bellum coquetry
and then falls silent, while a bronze
Silenus, patron of these lawns,
lies riddled like a pepper box.

Ezra Pound at the Hôtel Jacob

Condemned to a red-plush room
    in a middle-class hotel
        in the decay of summer,

here prowls the polylingual,
    refractory, irrepressible
        archenemy of convention—

red fox-muzzle beard, red dressing gown—
    and growls at his guest while affably
        scratching himself.

"London," he ruminates, "New York,
    can't thinkably live in 'em.
        Provence might do.

"When I was in villeggiatura . . ."

The afternoon droops like a hot candle.
    Sweat beads on spectacles
        slither like melted tallow.

Only, from the couch where he sprawls back,
    indomitable that obelisk of beard
        admonishes the heavens.

The Beach at Palavas

Under a multitude of suns
the sand turns molten white and stabs
the soles of all the naked feet
that move across the beach like crabs.

Over the feet are rudely piled
mountainous bellies, breasts in billows.
Triangular uncovered hams
shine white beneath red beach-umbrellas.

The sky is prudent and demure;
checked blue and white, a dimity,
it watches crimson bathing suits
affront the cobalt of a sea

where bathers hop across the waves
agilely, aimlessly, like fleas.
This is, if you consult a map,
the sea that washed the shores of Greece,

from which came riding on the spume
Venus Anadyomene,
and other Venuses descend
up to their, in a word, the sea.

It smells much less of salt than sweat.
Give me a salt-sweaty kiss,
Serena, take my hand and wade
into the sea as warm as piss.

Still Life

Here on the table, a great scarred loaf of bread,
a cheese, a napkin checkered white and red,

a glass half-filled, a bottle black with wine,
a cream-white china bowl, a tangerine,

a water bottle bellied like a tun,
a yellow cup behind the bottle peeping,

and each of them without a shadow sleeping
in the winter light of the Mediterranean sun.

Here too I drowse, immersed in the design
made by the water flask, the bread, the wine,

and the dropped napkin, wishing I were able
to sleep under the sun, translucent as

the colored liquid sleeping in a glass;
to merely be, like bottles on a table.

A Smoke of Birds

Starlings descend at nightfall, wheeling and swarming round
a bamboo copse or a cedar of Lebanon.

They cross the face of the winter sun like a smoke.

A smoke of descending starlings: it takes the form succes-
sively of a ball, a hoop, a mandolin (or maybe a gui-
tar), a string of frankfurters, a candy poke

that swells to a balloon and then collapses with a hiss of
escaping gases.

Out of an emptiness is heard the chittering of birds.

Carnaval in the Midi

O masked ladies, excited with your dancing,
exuding Quelques Fleurs and your own perfume,
why do you dissipate the smoky quiet
of this café, its meditative gloom?
Now they have turned the lights on in the room.

Why do you rouse the waiter without pity?
Why does your laughter make me younger and older?
Why do your eyes declare that they are pretty
(beauty would calm me) , and why throw confetti
to settle on the broadcloth of my shoulder?

    What is my name?
I think I was contented till you came.

If once we were abandoned to each other
in some close-smelling room above the bar,
we could look out the window in the evening
after a rain and see some rain-washed star
wrung clean as our exhausted bodies are.

    Wisdom is passion's fruit.
    I am too proud, too timid,
but know there is a secret, an abstraction,
call it a soul, beneath the business suit,
a something that takes flight as evening falls
out of the bustle you bring to this café,
    alone, to watch the day
stretch out sleepily on the hill above the Public Garden;
to watch a sunset fade on stucco walls,
    and twilight harden,

and gas lamps nod like yellow parasols
under the sycamores, and bats take wing.

The equestrian statue of Louis, the Sun King,
stares at an arch erected in his honor.

Two Swans

One morning during Carnaval they found two swans in the
   Public Gardens, their necks twisted, their bodies side
   by side under an evergreen magnolia

not yet in flower, and nobody would ever know who killed
   them, whether a drunkard, whether a crazy artist,
   whether an old man tired of women's bodies and eager
   to destroy

a more impeccable beauty, or was he young (a domino
   bends over them, black with white moons for buttons,
   while the sky like a domino bends vastly over).

It was a crime of passion; if I have read

of other passionate crimes in curtained alcoves, knife or
   poison, they seemed less tragic than those two dead
   swans, Racinian victims, or the formal pool, empty
   without them, an eye of death that stares

fixedly into a fixed and empty sky.

The Peppermint Gardens

A beauty it has that pleases some,
this country sliced into even squares
of peppermint candy by garden walls,
with fruit trees leaning against the walls
like so many ladders, pear and plum,
each fruit plucked off before it falls—

an ordered beauty that having seen
for two long years, I choose to question,
tired of a too, too brilliant green,
too brilliant whites against the green.
Maybe from eating their plums I have
more than a twinge of indigestion,

and so find nothing to praise about
those geometrical rows of plum trees,
wanting a country where briars sprout
under the crazily twisted gum trees,
an imprecise, untutored country
where all the gardens are inside out.

In my country the big pines grow
  at the edge of the woods,
  in the heart of the woods,
wherever the autumn winds may plant them,
not in close order, row by row,
where acres are left that men will grant them,
and in my country the chestnut trees
scatter their harvest where they please.

About my country is nothing grand:
three gothic hills in lower case,
two valleys you could hold in your hand,
a church, a crossroad store, a school
standing no higher than your face,
a trout stream—so I catalogue
the magic of my country:
item, a grove of hickory,
item, a tumbledown factory,
item—damn my memory,
you must imagine the rest.

But sometimes when the candles sputter,
their trees, disordered by the utter
black placelessness of midnight, wail
like those of my own country;
and sometimes when in bed I see
three hills against the canopy,
three mischievous little hills that lie
side by side in a narrow bed,
kicking their feet against a muslin sky.

Voices from Home: 1923

> Fresh from the factory.
> Watch their eyes open!
> Are you covered?

Are you the ten-pin or the ball? How fast do you
think? Is your body ten years older than you are?
Do you like fine things?

> Are you covered?

> You and your family need it now.
> *You and your family need it now.*
> YOU AND YOUR FAMILY NEED IT NOW!

Are you covered?

Good to the last drop. The sort of girl you stop to look at.
Makes the easiest way the best way. The sunshine of the night.
From the sheep's back to yours. A handy place to throw trash.
Keeps you warm as toast. No metal can touch you.

> Are you covered?

(give her the gift you'd like to
get if not on sale in your vicinity
write for complete catalog and you
will avoid imitations and substitutes
if you are covered)

> Relax tense nerves.
> I like fine things and
> my body is ten years older.
> A handy place to throw trash?
> A handy place to throw trash.

> Good-by old flannel lining, good-by.
> Old flannel lining, good-by.

IV   The City of Anger

NOTE

When the exiles straggled home at last, they were met by no reporters, no cameramen, no official committee of welcome. The police launch lay moored to its dock and the pigeons fed peaceably in City Hall Park. Still, as we rode to our anonymous lodgings, a dozen old newspapers flapped like banners of greeting in the autumn wind.

We unpacked our luggage, slept, and emerged on the morning streets. Allagazam, allagazam, the great show is about to begin. The fire trucks dizzily skidding, the journey through mammoth caves, the jazz of riveting hammers, the death-defying leap from beam to beam on the fiftieth story. Allagazam, step up. See the genuine hoodlums, the old pretzel women, the African village, the businessmen dictating to three secretaries and a dictaphone. Come out with the crowd tonight, aw, be a sport. . . . He's crooked, I tell you. They're all crooks in this racket. Don't listen to the guy, he'll gyp you.

New York, inhabited by six million strangers, was the metropolis of curiosity and suspicion. It was the city without landmarks, the home of lasting impermanence, of dynamic immobility. It was the seat of violent emotions, hate, desire, exultance, and contempt, all momently changing at the tips of the nerves. It was the city of anger . . . but underneath the anger was another mood that some of us shared, a longing for utter ruin, a feeling of timeless melancholy, dry, reckless, defeated, and perverse.

Three Songs for Leonora

[And for Peggy Baird]

1. *Circus in Town*

Allaga*zam*,
the princess with bobbed hair who rides
the rump of the bay mare.
Allagazam, the gilded charioteers,
the pink hyena, and also a little girl
making water behind the lilac bushes.

Allagazam,
the princess said and opened
her arms. Her eyes said, "Take me."
But I am in love, Madame,
with three eccentric dancers.
The steam calliope
played Annie Laurie.

Allagazam,
Allallagazam,
see the fat lady,
see the bearded lady,
see the lady with two heads,
only twenty-five cents,
only the fourth part
of allagazam,

allagazam. Either our world
outmeasures us or we have grown
too epical for the day.
Who is your tailor?

What is the time, Mr. Cowley,
by last year's calendar?

2. *Dumbwaiter Song*

Leonora, I have rented an apartment,
bath, kitchenette, electric, telephone.
Come hang your best pajamas in the closet,
Leonora, I am lording there alone.

I will show you in an album, Leonora,
my relatives departed long ago,
also a genuine oleograph of Jesus
blessing communion bread by radio.

In the morning I will make you toast and coffee,
Leonora, I will do the shopping later.
I will bring you back asparagus in a taxi,
    my heart on the dumbwaiter.

Leonora O'Mara, my bowels yearn after you.
I will carry you my kidneys in a toaster,
    my brains in a chafing dish,
    my hand on a wicker tray,
Leonora la mina, O nora malina.
But Leonora wailed and went away.

3. *Tennessee Blues*

I met her in Chicago and she was married.
    Dance all day,
leave your man, Sweet Mamma, and come away;
manicured smiles and kisses, to dance all day, all day.
    How it was sad.

Please, Mr. Orchestra, play us another tune.

My daddy went and left me and left the cupboard bare.
Who will pay the butcher bill now Daddy isn't there?
  Shuffle your feet.
Found another daddy and he taught me not to care,
  and how to care.
Found another daddy that I'll follow anywhere.
  Shuffle your feet, dance,

dance among the tables, dance across the floor,
slip your arm around me, we'll go dancing out the door,
Sweet Mamma, anywhere, through any door.
Wherever the banjos play is Tennessee.

Buy 300 Steel

[*For Matthew Josephson*]

Buy 300 steel at the
market, buy 300 steel
at the market, buy 300
steel.

His face melted into the telephone,
his lips curled with hello, and dreamed
his vulcanized-rubber eyes,

with a hello . . . there was a lake beneath
the Bowling Green 6000 trees,
and hello, Bowling Green, the noise of waters

under a curdled sky, hello,
I dove into the lake, hello,
into the lake as green, hello,
as Mr. Kahn, hello, hello,
as green as Bowling Green.

I'll make a note of it, good-by, and rain
suddenly falling, down fell railways, coppers,
motors, industrials, Rebecca Steel,
Calumet, Monkey-Ward, and Chrysler falling,
rain steadily falling, public utilities
. . . always a good buy,

a good, I'll make a note of it,
buy, good-by, good-by.

The Eater of Darkness

[*For Robert M. Coates*]

Dipping an adroit hand into his hat, he found excessively
a patent razor, gin, a banjo-ukulele,

five cigar bands, 3-in-1, a jackknife with broken blades, a
portable bathtub, and a Sunday *Times,* as well as freck-
les, Matisse, red hair, a blue airplane, and a white rabbit.

The last he gave to the White Queen, who ran away.

The red-haired man burst into genuine tears, they did not
change to pearls. He went to a dance in Harlem. Holding a toy pistol bang to his head, he crumpled boom to
the floor, in time with Duke Ellington's umpah-umpah.

It was what everybody expected. That year everybody was
being baroque and outrageous, with a false hint of sad-
ness underneath. The parties were wonderful and nobody believed in them any more.

But the bullets were real and the death was real, I couldn't
get over it.

The Flower in the Sea

[For Hart Crane]

Jesus I saw, crossing Times Square
with John the Beloved, and they bade me stop;
my hand touched theirs.

Visions from the belly of a bottle.

The sea, white, white,
the flower in the sea,
the white fire glowing in the flower;
and sea and fire and flower one,
the world is one, falsehood and truth
one, morning and midnight, flesh and vision
one.

I fled along the boulevards of night
interminably and One pursued
—my bruised arms in His arms nursed,
my breast against His wounded breast,
my head limp against His shoulder.

The Narrow House

[For Kenneth Burke]

I found a seed and planted it.
A tree sprang up, I tended it,
through the dry summer watered it.
The apples ripened in the fall.

I broke the apples open, and I found
what I expected, only the ash of days.

The garden was rich and blighted.
Weeds overran the strawberry bed.
A woodchuck burrowed under the wall.
I sat alone in the dark kitchen
and watched the calendar.
     But wait,

wait!
  Something is waiting and hidden,
magnificent kisses, everlasting fame,
around the corner of next week, between
the edges of two days.

     Wait only,
I shall heap your lap with pears,
oranges, nectarines, and rubies;
shall weave for you a chain of afternoons
as golden as the world at your feet.

He waits,
  a tense man in a narrow house,
always asking too much, expecting only,
like ashes out of the sky, a rain of days.

The Turning of the Year

[*For Peter Blume*]

The year swings over slowly, like a pilot
southward now driving from the cold and dark
toward vertical suns and days of briefer twilight
and lamps less promptly lighted in the park;

more definite nights, and days more sharply ending.
How shrouded, empty of voice the streets appear
in these December dusks, their skies distending
till snow falls at the turning of the year.

Only in a dead city one man waking,
who tried to read the city by the glow
of towers feebly luminous and seeking
God in the skies grown suddenly bright with snow;

who listened till he heard the city speaking
in mortuary whispers to the snow.

Memphis Johnny

[*For Nathan Asch*]

They carry him off in a one-horse hack,
and he won't be thinking of coming back;

they CARry him off in a ONE-horse hack,
and he WON'T be thinking of COMing back,

may God have mercy upon his soul.
They dump his bones in a six-foot hole,

they shovel dirt on his open eyes,
and dirt clump-clumping against his thighs.

The dirt clumps down, the pebbles drum on his belly. A
morsel of sod hides the left nipple of his breast, and
crumbs of gravel seeping into the stiff interstices of his
limbs,

and worms crawl out, and worms crawl in,
and worms crawl out, and worms crawl in,

and worms crawl out, and one is feeling overwrought, quite
naturally so, forgetting that he wears such linen as he
never owned, and a suit of decent black, and glass, oak,
metal protecting his body from the soil. From the
worms. And, yes, it is a natural delusion to imagine
oneself within the glass, oak, metal, clutching his shoulders tightly or pursuing a pointless conversation round
and about,

while dirt clump-clumps against my thighs,
against my belly and frozen eyes,

against my shoulder, my breast, my knees,
and shovelsful of eternities,

and worms crawl in, and worms crawl out,
and round and round and upon and about
our pointless conversation grows,
and there she goes,
                    and there she goes,
and alldressedup in her Sunday clothes—
                    and there she goes.

Tumbling Mustard

[For Harold Loeb]

Born in a fence corner,
raised in a coulee,
married in Nebraska,
parted on the Sound:
They call me Tumbling Mustard, "Hey, Tumbling Mustard, what's your business, listen Buddy, where are you
bound?"

Monday in Omaha,
Tuesday in Dakota,
one day in Memphis,
three in Allentown:
Mud roads and stony roads, concrete and macadam; she
would never leave me if I would settle down.

Columbine and larkspur,
peony and dahlia,
cornflower, mayflower,
each has a place:
I am the tumbleweed that rolls across the prairies, winds at
the back of it, mountains in its face.

Tumbleweed, tumbleweed,
riding his velocipede,
east side, west side,
all around the moon:
Denver, San Francisco, Winnipeg and Dallas, maybe if the
gas holds out we'll get there soon.

The Lady from Harlem

[In memory of Florence Mills]

The fetish woman crossed the stage,
her limbs convulsed with yellow magic.
Art is the gratuitous
shiver that makes the shimmy tragic.
Obeah, obeah, wailed the saxophones.

Though orchestras play Dixie Dreams,
never in Dixie field was picked
the guncotton that swells your breast,
explodes, and leaves me derelict
amid the wreckage of your smile,

floating over the parterre.
Your sudden fingers touched my wrist.
Tell me, did Madam Walker do your hair
before she died in Tarrytown
among her butlers, footmen, chefs?

Throned on a tomb of brass you reign
between the bass and treble clefs.

Restaurateur with Music

Knishes, kisses,
white wine and seltzer.
Good evening, ladies,
says the Original
Moscowitz.

My father read the Talmud,
my mother wore a wig,
my mother looked at a gipsy,
I play the cymbalon.

Ai, ai, business is bad
at night under the paper roses.
Art in America, ai, ai.

Commemorative Bronze
1928

EVERY MAN HIS OWN ROBESPIERRE ** IT WAS THE
FIRST DAY OF THE YEAR ONE ** LEGISLATIVE
POWER HAD BEEN SEIZED BY ACTORS EQUITY **
JUDICIARY POWER BY THE ADVERTISING MENS
POST OF THE AMERICAN LEGION ** WHICH BECAME
A COMMITTEE OF PUBLIC SAFETY ** DEATH TO THE
WOWSERS DEATH ** THE MAYOR DIED UNDER THE
WHEELS OF THE LEXINGTON AVENUE EXPRESS **
THE POLICE WERE JAILED TO THE LAST MAN **
THE COMMISSIONER OF THE PORT WAS DROWNED
** POETS WERE HANGED IN CLUSTERS FROM THE
LAMPPOSTS ** UNDER THE SMALL BRIGHT LEMON
COLORED STARS ** ALL AVENUES DURING THE EX-
ECUTIONS ** WERE LUMINOUS WITH RED ORANGE
YELLOW GREEN BLUE INDIGO AND DAYLIGHT
BULBS ** FURNISHED BY COURTESY OF THE NEW
YORK EDISON COMPANY ** BROADWAY WAS CLOSED
TO TRAFFIC ** THERE WERE JAZZ BANDS AT THE
CORNERS OF EVEN NUMBERED STREETS ** OFTEN
WE DANCED NAKED AT THE BURNING OF A CHURCH
** UNDER CRIMSON SKIES ** IN THE GUTTERS
THAT OVERFLOWED ** WITH URINE **
BLOOD ** AND WINE

Those of Lucifer

[For Allen Tate]

Out of an empty sky the dust of hours;
a word was spoken and a folk obeyed;
an island uttered incandescent towers
like frozen simultaneous hymns to Trade.

Here in a lonely multitude of powers,
thrones, dominations, celestial cavalcade,
they rise
          —proclaiming Sea and sky are ours,
and yours, O man, the shadow of our shade.

Or, did a poet crazed with dignity
rear them upon an island to prolong
his furious contempt for sky and sea?
To what emaciated hands belong
those index fingers of infinity?

O towers of intolerable song!

Ten Good Farms

[For Slater Brown]

With storm-washed gullies marking where the streets
ran riverward, with mounds of splintered glass
and barricades of marble spilt across them
and crazy girders bridging them, to rust
   in the northeast gales;

with towers crumbling in the sunshine, lakes
of peace in every cellar, brambles guarding
the public squares, and underfoot a rat
crossing the stone jungle (all horizons
   vast and empty of smoke) ;

no, in our lifetime we could never make
out of Manhattan Island ten good farms,
or five, or two—and yet the open graveyards,
the rich plots where slaughterhouses flourished
and one day fell—our gardens will be there.

V   The Dry Season

NOTE

By 1930 or thereabouts we were men on the threshold of
middle age, each with a household to support. We had ceased
to be a generation of friends inscribing poems to one another,
and of sometimes bitter rivals united by their distrust of older
persons; instead we were busy with our separate jobs. Hurry,
the printer is waiting, the letter must go out, the important
visitor is coming at four o'clock. Hurry or you will miss the
Washington train. It was exciting to have a share in the business of the world, perhaps in shaping its future, but some of
us came to feel that we were not dealing with persons any
longer; there was no time for that. More and more we dealt
with categories and convenient abstractions: the Economist,
the Agronomist, the China Hand, the Young Writer Needing
Encouragement. And wasn't it possible that we too had become
mere functions printed in large type (as in later times they
would be punched) on stiff cards not to be spindled or kissed:
the Journalist, the Editor, the Faculty Wife, the Government
Official?

From those years I remember looking for simple emotions
that would, at any cost, reassure me that I lived. There was not
much time for writing poems, less even than for truly personal
relations, but I tried to say in all simplicity that black is black,
that love is good, and that home is something you can never go
back to. What I feared most and sometimes detected was a dry-
ness of the heart.

This Morning Robins

Yesterday snow, piled high on the black branches;
this morning robins where the snow had perched,
frogs peeping in the swamp, woodchucks alert
beside their holes, the sentinels of spring.

In hip boots the fishermen slouch by,
thinking with nervous wrist a first clean cast,
a first hard strike. The plowman's daily eyes
that follow them are pale as trout-swirled water.

How many springs outlived, how many suns
from clouds outburrowing like April woodchucks,
how many plans for the ripe corn! And the flowers
frost-fallen in how many autumns! Tell me,
swamp peepers, meadow robins, tell me now
    how many springs?

The Dry Season

I climbed the mountain, to its inmost crags
    I climbed and found no rain,
only the steady dry southwester there,
beating and bending the sea-green hemlock boughs.

    No squirrel sang there,
nor fawn's foot rustled the early-fallen leaves,
nor partridge boasting in the underbrush
    drummed on a log.

    The springs were dry,
the stream bed stony there, its pools half-stagnant,
with snakes beside them dozing and the trout
gasping and dying at the water's brim.

    A man was there
who prayed for rain, who danced for rain, who sang,
aiyee, the lightning splits the skies apart
and rain pours out of them, *aiyee*, the meadow
dances with corn, the mountain sings with rain.

    His voice died out
there in the wind, among the sun-bleached stones
    and the sun-dried air.

Sing if you must, old friend, dance if you will;
this month will bring no answer to your prayer.
It is August, the dry season of your life.
Take out your heart and wring it between your hands;
no pain will dart, no blood will drip from it.
    No blood is there.

The Mother

It was a noon of freedom,
an afternoon in chains,
and we have shared them, mother,
who fed me from your veins.

It was a long day's labor
that had no evening rest.
Sleep, can you sleep now, mother,
as once the babe at breast,

as once the babe within you,
sleep in the womb of earth?
Oh, take my blessing, mother,
for all I knew since birth:

sunlight and shadow, freedom
and prison, feast and dearth.
The cord was strong that bound us,
now binding me to earth.

The Firstborn

What can I offer you now, now?
Heavy the years pass over me. How
  give you the freight of them,
  spare you the weight of them?

What have I learned for you here, here?
What have I saved for you, made for you? Where
  the word to pass on to you
  with my blood gone to you?

Only the rain beating now and the trees dim in the air.

The Long Voyage

Not that the pines were darker there,
nor mid-May dogwood brighter there,
nor swifts more swift in summer air;
   it was my own country,

having its thunderclap of spring,
its long midsummer ripening,
its corn hoar-stiff at harvesting,
   almost like any country,

yet being mine; its face, its speech,
its hills bent low within my reach,
its river birch and upland beech
   were mine, of my own country.

Now the dark waters at the bow
fold back, like earth against the plow;
foam brightens like the dogwood now
   at home, in my own country.

The Man of Promise

The well-bred children, the well-clipped grass,
the well-served dinner, the low-pitched laugh,
the open bottle, the ice in the glass
   —not, nowhere, nobody, nothing.

The job well done, the books in the black,
the doorman's greeting, the steward's bow,
the hearty handshake, the slap on the back
   —not, nowhere, nobody, nothing.

The breathless meeting, the kiss in the hall,
the door unlocked and locked again,
all night the shadow on the wall
   —not, nowhere, nobody, nothing.

Bed and bottle and bread and birth,
laughing and longing and late and lorn,
the faded flowers, the fresh-turned earth
   —not, nowhere, nobody, nothing.

Tar Babies

Young Mr. Androgyne, the talented poet,
pours out in verse his, oh, how lovely soul.
—My body is as lovely as my verse,
big truckdriver, if you like this verse of mine,
take me, big truckdriver.

Mr. Dorante calls Joyce by his first name,
has taken lunch with Gide, knows Eliot.
                              —Oh,
how sweet the pollen of genius on my lips
that kiss the hands of the great!
                              —Meet Mr. Dorante.

And Mr. Slick the critic has complained
about the unmannerly ways of other critics,
but suavely, in a style that creeps across
your cheeks like a barber's fingers.
                              —Haircut,
Mister?
          —shave, Mister?
                              —singe, tonic, shampoo?

Pride, scorn, O selfless and divine Anger,
let me in your white violence take refuge,
washed clean of calculation. Let me die
cursing in a corner. They are many.
Is murder certainly a crime?

Weakness is crime, hating is crime.
Don't hit the tar baby, keep your hands clean of him.
Don't hit the tricky sticky baby.

Ernest

Safe is the man with blunderbuss
who stalks the hippopotamus
on Niger's bank or scours the veldt
to rape the lion of his pelt;

but deep in peril he who sits
at home to rack his lonely wits
and there do battle, grim and blind,
against the jackals of the mind.

Roxane

. . . was Flatbush born, was twenty-six,
had lavender eyes and frizzly hair.
A Dutchman got her in a fix
in Carcassonne. A pockmarked Swede
took her to Budapest by air.

And she was bored, Roxane, Roxane
was talented and incomplete.
I knew her when an Englishman
was keeping her in two dull rooms
on a dead-end street.

I knew her too when sick with love
or lovelessness or womankind
she closed her lavender eyes and dove
into the river bright with gulls,
used condoms, turds, and grapefruit rind,

thought better of it, swam to shore.
I too have plunged into that sea
of filth, and thought that nevermore
should I swim landward, yet I died,
and lived, no more than she.

The Lost People

The bedroom on the courtyard and the tree
of heaven that brushed the window there—we slept
and loved and slept away the afternoon;
the quiet in the streets and twilight still
at ten o'clock, the sidewalk tables crowded,
the Arab selling rugs, and we moved south,
south with the end of summer to a shore
that looked to Africa, and fleshly white
    sea-lilacs died in the sand.

Then north again with spring, the wooden inn
dry-rotting under the Heiterwand, the major
without a pension, fragile and polite,
full-breasted Rosa singing to the starved
and pederastic poet, these were broken
wax figures in a wax-pale landscape. We
were new, invincible, we paid our bills
and then moved on. A moment to admire
the glister of decay, and we moved on
    brightly among the ruins.

Late, late in youth we heard the market wagons
roll in the streets, the blind violinist play,
but did we hear the shamble of the waiter
coming to count our saucers, did we hear
the shots, the hobnailed echoes die away?
And bedward stumbling did we understand,
at daybreak with our sweethearts, that we should
at evening waken in a furnished room
    somewhere, alone and old?

The way is long. Insensitivity
is vice. "Why not?" is vice. The tepid lovers
forsaken in each other's beds, the habit
of little treacheries, the friends unliked,
the joyless orgy, these and these are vice.
From fields as green as jellied mint, from houses
bright as our toys, substantial as our fathers,
we sailed against the sun and found ourselves
here in a countryside of phlegm-gray mist
    and soot-gray shadowless evil.

Is it too late for homeward journeys? Prince,
Archangel, Satan, what we ask is only
a word to unlock the corridors of dream.
Lest in the wilderness of days we wander
too long without direction, take our hands,
close tight our eyes, and lead us into nights
rich with the smell of childhood. Life is heavy
on our bent shoulders. Lift the burden, Prince,
and gently guide us toward the mother darkness,
    the solacing arms of the tomb.

Seven

I woke and could not see the familiar white
walls of my bedroom, somewhere woke and dreamed
that crabwise I was climbing a long stair
toward what I did not know, or whom, but always,
backward and sideward, step by step I climbed,
till under me I saw a burning town—

my town and house, my lifetime, my desires.
I dreamed and I was climbing a long stair
rising toward emptiness. A voice cried, "Seven
is waiting there." I knew that Seven was
my fate and God, that Seven was a sphere
on a tall throne resting. Seven was an eye

that watched my progress, fisherlike and cold.
"I have been idle, Seven," and the voice
was mine that murmured, "Seven, I have been
self-centered, self-indulgent," but there came
no answer on the steps where still I climbed.
"Help me, have pity on me, Seven." Now

the answering voice was in me but not mine.
"Climb on," it said, "climb to that sideward height
where Seven is waiting, Seven eternally
there, by nothing surrounded, nothing beneath,
nothing above. The goal. The nethermost answer.
The white egg-shaped motionless, speechless No."

VI   The Unsaved World

NOTE

He stands in a long, hot, smoky room in Yorkville, facing an audience uncomfortably seated on rows of folding chairs. Everyone there is shabby, though a few have the look of being dressed in old clothes merely for the occasion. He wants to remind them all of the millions who have died for the cause, some in every country of the world, including—he mentions two names—our own. "Those dead are fighting on our side," he says in a low voice, but with conviction.

"Louder, louder!" somebody shouts from the back of the room.

Raising his voice, he speaks of those who draw aside from the battle, retiring to the safety of their . . . ivory towers. He is ashamed of using the phrase. Everything he says is what he deeply feels to be true, but there are reservations that he keeps to himself; they could never be expressed in the phrases that his audience waits to recognize and applaud. "Why can't I speak in my own voice?" he wonders as he raises a clenched fist and waits for the last hand-clap before sitting down in his folding chair.

He goes home alone through streets that are still pleasantly cool from an evening shower. Walking as if to music, he thinks of being not a leader, but merely a soldier ready to die for a new society. Comrades marching shoulder to shoulder. That night, however, he dreams his old obsessive dream of climbing a long stairway, then another, then another, and of standing at last in an empty place, guilty and isolated, before a white egg-shaped motionless, speechless No.

For St. Bartholomew's Eve

August 23, 1927

Then die!
           Outside the prison gawk
the crowds that you will see no more.
A door slams shut behind you. Walk
with turnkeys down a corridor
smelling of lysol, through the gates
to where a drunken sheriff waits.

St. Nicholas who blessed your birth,
whose hands are rich with gifts, will bear
to you no further gifts on earth,
Sacco, whose heart abounds in prayer
neither to Pilate nor a saint
whose earthly sons die innocent.

And you that never for God's grace
once pleaded, black Bartholomew,
no God will raise you from this place
nor Virgin intercede for you,
nor bones of yours make sweet the plot
where governors and judges rot.

A doctor sneezes, A chaplain maps
the roads of heaven. You mount the chair.
A jailer buckles tight the straps
like those that aviators wear.
The surgeon makes a signal.
                      Die!
lost symbols of our liberty.

Beyond the chair, beyond the bars
of day and night your path lies free,
a windswept avenue of stars.
March on, O dago Christs, while we
march on to spread your names abroad
like ashes in the winds of God.

The Last International

I saw them, yes, I saw their unbreathing armies
marching against the Capitol in ranks
that filled the boulevard from curb to curb;
they were a river high between its banks

in the March gales. I saw their featureless faces
wax-pallid, saw their tight-clenched bony fists,
saw their right forearms skyward raised, and saw
among them stumps of arms, hacked off at the wrists.

And some I saw that walked in a frozen circle
of flame, and some had snapped-off bayonets
in their ribs, and some a wound between the shoulders
from which the blood congealed in two black jets.

And some there were and some I saw that carried
in their left hands each his own dissevered head,
and others wearing still a hangman's noose
that marched among those armies of the dead—

for comrades dead, for having loved tomorrow,
betrayed and bastinadoed, burned at the stake,
slow-starved in prison or exile, buried alive,
beaten insensible, roused at the day's break,

then hurried through the snow to execution,
shot down in Florisdorf or Chapei Road,
and now reprieved from prison graveyards piled
so high with sorrows that they overflowed,

yes, poured their victims out, a long parade
of specters high upborne on rivers of air
and silence. Not a banner flapped in the wind.
There was only the dry whisper everywhere

of feet like dry leaves over asphalt scudding
under a cold sky heavy as a vault
and the slit eyes of iron-shuttered windows,
and suddenly were voices crying, Halt!

I heard them, living voices that were more
unhuman than the silence of the dead.
In terror, in a dream, I turned and saw them
waiting, the gas-masked, shrapnel-helmeted,

identical brown frozen bodies, heard
the click of rifle bolts behind barbed wire,
and turning back I pleaded,
                               "Comrades, not
weaponless, not to crumple under fire.

"No farther, comrades—"
                          Would they hear me ever?
"Stand here."
                But still they moved to the attack,
until the enemy ordnance volleyed out
against them an enormous thundercrack.

And still and still the mutineers marched on
with mummified limbs that bullets could not tear,
nor gases poison them, who did not breathe,
nor tanks crush out their bodies that were air.

I saw them sweeping forward, saw the soldiers
that cast their rifles down and blindly fled;

barons I saw and bankers and archbishops
driven before the whirlwind of the dead;

stone walls that crumbled, barracks and asylums
fast emptied, penitentiaries ablaze.
An unchoked sigh, a moan of liberation
rose from mean streets and moonless areaways,

from factory gates and convict camps and cabins
unpainted, windowless, deep in the Cotton Belt;
tensed muscles loosening, a first free breath
a hundred million times repeated, felt

then slowly heard, tornado of the mind,
driving the mist and terror from the head.
The vault of cloud was split by a sharp wind.
The sky was suddenly blue and the sun shone red.

1935

Tomorrow Morning

Tomorrow, walking in the dew-bright fields
or singing with your voices pitched above
the blackbird's chuckle, tomorrow when you scheme
to break new records, raise production, then
think back on us. Mechanics of the morning,
you of the blunt hands, the sensitive fingers,
think back on us, remember these dry bones,
earth-yellow, not a word of us in the textbooks
—our graves, even, marked by no white stones.

Think back on us who argued through the night
in a closed and crowded room, our voices low,
and spies who listened through the thin partitions
and traitors in the midst of us. Think back
on us who quarreled there, hating each other
more than the enemy, our cigarettes
burned down to the last half-inch, our faces gray
under the stubble. Then the lights went out.
We heard machine guns tapping yesterday.

Think back on us who poured into the streets
cold in the dawn twilight, peopled with
mechanical voices screeching out their lies
into the mist, and airplanes overhead:
confusion, rumor spreading from the skies.
A corpse was sprawled on the cathedral steps
—ours, for I knew his features in the beam
of a pocket torch. And now their riflemen
came slinking like the creatures of a dream,

crouching in doorways, always nearer. We
must rouse the labor unions, we must warn
the Central Committee. But the wires are down,
the streets are barricaded, the doors bolted
against us in a suddenly hostile town.
Too late to cry for help, too late to scurry
into safe hiding now. Across the broad
dim plaza, from the bull-ring by the river,
rises the rattle of the firing squad.

Think back on us, mechanics of tomorrow,
breakers of records, riders of the spray,
swimmers of air, think back on us who died
at Badajoz, like beasts in the arena,
in Canton, cornered in an alleyway.
Think back on us, the martyrs and the cowards,
the traitors even, swept by the same flood
of passion toward the morning that is yours:

O children born from, nourished with our blood.

1937

Eight Melons

August. On the vine eight melons sleeping,
drinking the sunlight, sleeping, while below,
their roots obscurely work in the dark loam;

motionless center of the living garden,
eight belly-shaped, eight woman-colored melons
swelling and feeding the seeds within them. Guns

west of the river at the Frenchman's Bridge;
they are fighting now at the cold river, they
are dying for tomorrow. While the melons

sleep, smile in sleeping, in their bellies hoard
September sweetness, life to outlast the snow.

1937

The End of the World

Not the harsh voice in the microphone,
not broken covenants or hate in armor,
  but the smile like a cocktail gone flat,
  the stifled yawn.

Not havoc from the skies, death underfoot,
the farmhouse gutted or the massacred city,
  but the so-nice couple retired on their savings,
  the weeded garden, the loveless bed.

House warm in winter, city free of vice,
tree that outstood the equinoctial gales,
  dry at the heart they crashed
  on a windless day.

1940

The Time of Crossword Puzzles

From the French (1940) of Louis Aragon

O sun of sleepless midnight, solitude
of husbandless houses where they lie awake,
spouses of terror, counting round their beds
the monsters that stand leering till daybreak.

Who was it that unchained the banished fear,
put sand on the roof, insomnia in their hearts,
and daubed the windowpanes with panic blue?
Nobody any more consults the cards.

Keep dancing, wizards, on your briary heath:
they will not seek your love-philtres again.
Love bowed their heads more humbly than a prayer
when the East Station swallowed up their men.

Women who know at last as we ourselves
the paradise lost of our unknotted limbs,
do you hear the voice that murmurs, Only you,
as lips bestow a kiss on the hollow winds?

Abominable absence, absinthe of the war:
once more we drink that bitter counterfeit,
and yet our limbs were fused not long ago;
I sensed for you whatever your body did.

Too little have we prized those double hours,
too little asked if our dreams were counterparts,
too seldom probed the look in troubled eyes,
too seldom talked of our concurrent hearts;

but only as a secret to share with you
do I see the world in its other countenance,
when rain clouds grizzle the aging face of day,
or now when midnight trees begin to dance.

Listen. In the night my heartbeats call.
I grope in bed for your presence unawares
and everything slips away. Except for you,
nothing else matters. I am not one of theirs.

I am not theirs because I should have to be
like Ligier's carved half-skeleton at Bar,
fleshless down to the waist, but holding up
to the high window his poor barbarous heart.

I am not theirs because my human flesh
is not a pastry to be cut with the knife;
because a river seeks and finds the sea;
because my living needs a sister life.

I am yours. I am yours only. I adore
your footprint and the hollow where you lay,
your lost slipper, your handkerchief. Go sleep,
my frightened child. I promise to lie awake

here until dawn. The medieval night
has draped this broken universe with black.
If not for us, the storm will some day pass.
The time of crossword puzzles will come back.

1944

Passport Blues

When I was a virgin
   I lived in a mansion;
Latin I studied and
   Sanskrit and scansion,
bright as the china on
   Grandmother's shelf.
Now I'm a widow,
ten times a widow,
never been married and
   live by myself.
Oh, honey, how long must I wait for a passport,
   wait for a visa, wait for a home?

From Bremen to Budapest,
Landeck to Liverpool,
   Scotland to Spain—
I left them by steamer,
   by truck and by train,
always a fugitive,
always suspected,
never convicted,
   nowhere to go.
I went to the consul;
   the consul said No.
Oh, honey, how long must I wait for a passport,
   wait for a visa, wait for a home?

Baggage and bedlinen,
   virtue and hope—
in Bremen I lost them,
future and family,

toothbrush and soap.
Then Bremen was only
weeds among stones;
with Grandmother's china
lay Grandfather's bones.
Oh, honey, how long must I wait for a passport,
wait for a visa, wait for a home?

My mother was blinded.
She sent me a cable:
Come home, little daughter,
come home to our cellar,
come starve at our table.
But who will sign papers
and who pay my fare
so far, so very far?
A home is wherever
you were and a hell
is wherever you are.
Oh, honey, how long must I wait for a passport,
honey, please find me a home.

1947

Ode in a Time of Crisis

—jumped over the quick brown fox
jumped over the lazy dog
jumped over now is the time
jumped over all good men and true
jumped into the party
   to save the party
   to save the nation

a grand old nation it was
a swell party at the best hotel

the birds and the beasts were there
the quick brown foxes were there
the lazy dogs were there
all good men and true were there
all right-thinking women

—the hot mammas and nincompapas
the big baboon by the light of the moon
the alligators, commentators
punks and investigators
the astors and top brasstards
colonel obtuse of the daily noose
luce and la puce and the holy goose
all came to the aid of the party
   and saved the party
   and saved the nation.

1951

The Enemy Within

Beware of snogs.
They penetrate everywhere.
They are rich in subterfuge and delation.
They whisper against you in a corner of your mind.

All evil comes from snogs.
Unmask them, drive them into stony places,
encircle them with stones and stone them dead,
so that the earth lies clean under God's clean eye
and is God's earth again.
                              Still, might it be
that a snog survives, a shadowy node of evil
among the justicers?

How tell a snog
in all his involute treachery, his disguise
hiding disguises? Only one rule is safe:
all the accused are guilty,
all the accused feel guilt in their hearts,
all stand accused, wife, mistress, lover, brother,
detective, criminal, judge, even yourself—

pursued by snogs to the last brink of darkness,
cornered, pushed backward, hurtled into the gulf
as into an ether sleep;
spinning, hearing their laughter spiral down,
already smelling the green death below,
yet hearing your own laughter spiral up
because of a last ironical doubt: was I
victim or priest? Myself was I

or wasn't I, was-wasn't in a faster
and faster downward spiral, wasn't I,
was, wasn't I a snog?

1952

Here with the Long Grass Rippling

1

I wonder—lying in the long grass
where ants are busy among the roots; half-watching them,
half-listening for the sound I used to hear in June, of stone
    on scythe—
I wonder if in every created species
a law inheres that drives it forward to its own destruction.

Fish, lizard, bird, or beast, they multiply;
they grow in strength or speed, in appetite, in simple bulk,
as nature sharpens their fangs or sheathes them in armor;
they cover the land, churn the seas white,
or gather in clouds that darken the sun for hours.
One morning,
whether eaten by enemies or by their own kind,
or starved by having wiped out the species on which they
    feed,
or parched or frozen by a change in the weather,
as if at a spoken word they vanish.

Here in the long grass that nobody has bothered to cut
since the cows were sold, I think of the wild cattle
that browsed the endless grasslands of northern Africa.
Did they increase till the grass was gnawed to the roots,
and the roots blew away,
and sand came drifting westward with the harmattan?

2

The great mammals are extinct or enslaved,
or tranquilized and tagged, then left to wander—

not widely, for now another species,
weak in itself, but having words for its fangs and armor,
swarms everywhere on earth.
It conquers by force of words,
and shields each conquest with words,
and dreams in words of being its own law.
But is it not wordlessly obeying the same law as all the
 others?

—increasing in numbers,
like the horned cattle of what used to be the North African
 prairies;
increasing in stature,
like the dinosaurs and the mastodons, each when their day
 was ending;
increasing in mobility,
till men outstrip the antelope and the humming bird and
 stare down at the eagle;
stare down at the earth itself as it spins in space;
while each of the new men
demands as much of its surface as a hundred did in the past,
and always more of its treasures,
till now his wastage litters the earth, corrupts the air, poi-
 sons the water.
Fire is his element,
and he burns his way forward remorselessly toward what?
in always more rapid progress toward what?

Here in the realm of ants,
here with the long grass rippling over my head,
I remember the affable biologist
who dreamed aloud, after the second martini,
"If we could only sterilize three billion people—
sterilize, vaporize, it doesn't matter,
so long as they included a high proportion of fertile women—

then the species could start over."
Yes, but only to move faster toward the same goal.

And the bombing pilot home from Vietnam:
"Of course," he said, "we burned a lot of towns.
We must have killed a lot of people.
But think how the others will go forward once the war is
    over,
with all those fields to reclaim, those towns to rebuild,
and all those machines they didn't have before."
He was a servant of progress,
but so are the rest of us, in peace or war,
each in his own fashion—
some of us saving or making possible ten lives
for every life that others destroy;
some of us creating new wants
that others ravage the earth to satisfy;
some of us fighting to save the earth from other saviors;
and most of us living as in a supermarket,
loading our carts so high that they spill over into mounds of
    garbage.
Healers, inventors, merchandisers, housewives,
are we not all soldiers of progress,
heralds of the last day?

    3

High overhead a plane moves westward,
inaudible, invisible, but leaving behind a vapor trail
as if God's finger had written a question or a warning;
while I, in the crushed, unvalued, precious grass,
and only for myself, offer a prayer.

I pray for this:
to walk as humbly on the earth as my father and mother did;

to greatly love a few;
to love the earth, to be sparing of what it yields,
and not to leave it poorer for my long presence;
to speak some words in patterns that will be remembered,
and again the voice be heard to exult or mourn—
all this, and in some corner where nettles grew in the black
    soil,
to plant and hoe a dozen hills of corn.

1968

VII   Another Country

. . . Michault,
Qui fut nommé le Bon Fouterre:
Priez pour luy, faictes ung sault:
A Saint-Satur gist, soubz Sancerre.

Stone Horse Shoals

"To wade the sea-mist, then to wade the sea
at dawn, let drift your garments one by one,
follow the clean stroke of a sea-gull's wing
   breast-high against the sun;
follow a sail to sunward, slowly nearing
the lazy lobster boats off Stone Horse Shoals,
and pass them silent, on a strong ebb-tide
into an ocean empty to the poles—"

The tall man clenched his eyes against the world;
his face was gray and shook like a torn sail.
"I have lived," he said, "a life that moved in spirals
turned inward like the shell of a sea-snail.
I have been the shadow at the heart of shadows;
I have stared too many years at my own face.
On Stone Horse Shoals, among the lobster boats,
   I will shed my carapace.

"Something will die there, something move and watch
its shadow fathoms downward on the sand,
summer and winter. In another season
another man comes wading to the land,
where other blossoms fade among the dunes
and other children. . . . I am tired," he said,
"but I can see a naked body climbing
a naked seacoast, naked of the dead,

"naked of language. There are signs inscribed
on stones and trees, familiar vocables;
I hope to rise out of the sea as white,

as empty and chalk-smooth as cockleshells.
And children digging naked in the sand
will find my shell and on it scratch new words
that soon will blossom out," he said, "and bear
new fruit, strange to the tongue of men and birds."

There Is a Moment

There is a moment after the embrace
when happily fatigued we do not speak,
when still my cheek is resting on your cheek,
when hearts throb still and limbs still interlace

under the coverlet. (Your lips are mild,
timeless and forgiving; your limp hand
rests for a moment on the pillow and
you watch me with the tired face of a child.)

There is a moment logical and white
behind the wall of flesh. It is as if,
falling agreeably from some high cliff,
we floated in a limitless sea of light

among impersonal forms, and came to rest
within the personal limits of a night
where chair and bed loom comfortably trite,
where still my heart is beating on your breast.

Leander

Un noyé pensif parfois descend.
—RIMBAUD

Between the waves, out of the sight of land,
at nightfall toward an unseen beacon swimming;
the sea flung her arms about his arms
in foam, mingled her hair with his,
    and clung against his breast;
against his lips the salt pulse of the sea.

"Leander, I will show you all my treasures,
caverns of pearl, Leander, constellations
of incandescent fish. Leviathan
my servant shall attend you, and my sharks
surround you in the armies of their splendor,
and octopi shall build a wall of arms:
    surrender to the sea."

The waves that lapped his shoulders cried, "Surrender,"
and dead men's bones a thousand fathoms under
called in their sterner voices, "O Leander,
    surrender."

He lingered to the rhythm of the waves,
a last time felt the rain against his cheek,
then slowly filled his lungs with water, sank
through immense halls of darkness, infinite
chambers of dream, a white thing that drifts
southward with the current, a cold body
    whittled by the sea.

    And Hero
waiting in her desolate chamber, Hero,
    be comforted;

for they have taken the dead whose flesh you loved
and dressed him in the plunder of the sea;
his hair is wreathed with algae; his eyes gleam
luminous with jellyfishes; coral
blooms on his thighs; his arms are braceleted
with pearl, and scars of kisses on his breast.

Regal and tired, O corpse that mapped the countries
of ocean, saw pelagic meadows where
the sea cow grazes, traveler who skirts
the unicellular gardens of the foam:
southward you drift, where archipelagoes
of stars deflect the current, and waters boil
with lava, through indefinite Marquesas,
whirling in the typhoon, and off Cape Stiff
in westerly gales your eyes commemorate,
still tropical, the wax and wane of moons.
Time is a secret frozen in your smile.

William Wilson

A man there is of fire and straw
consumed with fire, whom first I saw
once at a dance, when nearer and nearer
there swirled a mist, and lights grew dim,
and I came face to face with him
outlined against me in a mirror.

As red as wine, as white as wine,
his face which is not and is mine
and apes my face's pantomime.
   It makes a threatening movement, halts,
and orchestras in perfect time
continue the Blue Danube Waltz.

He makes a movement and retires,
this man of straw and many fires,
Iago doubled with Othello.
   Often I startle up in bed
to find him lying there, my fellow.
   Often I wish that he were dead,
and hack him often, skin and bone,
and dreaming often, hear my own
life's blood drip on the crumpled pillow,

where once, immortal as a stone,
true love lay strangled by Othello.

The Living Water

In the hot afternoon,
in the burned meadow,
the brook is a bloodstain dried
black on the dry gray stones.

In the hot afternoon,
in the hillside pasture,
climb where the water flowed
last spring, there is life beyond

the broken fence, in the locust grove,
there is water standing in pools
and a kingfisher darting over
the minnows trapped for his feast.

Climb on and find the ravine.
Crickets are silent there,
but over a breast-high ledge
is heard the trickle of water.

The banks are steeper (climbing),
the shade is deeper (stumbling),
the pools are deeper (climbing),
and here they are empty of minnows.

See, in their depths at last
the arrowlike shadows of trout.

In the hot afternoon, from the hillside pasture,
climb to find water, stumbling into the gorge,
climbing beyond to the vine-entangled swamp,

where catbriars hide the brook that now runs deep
and trout are cool in their sunless kingdom. Climb,
stumble and climb, for the source of it all is here—

here the final and secret pool,
with green scum at the edge of it,
a cloud of midges over it,
and bubbling from the depths of it,
stirring the frogs' eggs and the fishes' eggs,
here the source, the limpid and living water
rising from white sand.

Natural History

1. *Piney Woods*

Teeth on the saw,
teeth on the rake,
trout in the brook,
pine in the brake—

The big trees sing to the little trees
   in the pine-crowded brake,
"Here is a twigful of sky," they sing,
"that we will stretch out our limbs and take.
Here is a seep of rain to drink
and rotting leaves to yeast our bread.
Give us the last of your earth," they sing,
   "that our great roots may spread."

Gorging on mould,
engrossing the sky,
the big trees grow.
The little trees die.

2. *The Silvery Fishes*

From the vast of it,
from summer fields pegged flat beneath the sky,
enormous sunlight blazing out of them,
   I hid myself away
under the water, under green water,
where silvery fishes nibbled at my thighs,
   and heard them saying:

"We swam upstream for three days and three nights,
for three days drifted southward with the current,
and nowhere found a limit to the world.
    It is shaped like a willow branch.
Heroes came forth, but none could ever swim
    to the tipmost leaf."

A kingfisher cast his shadow on the water.
The fishes hid away beneath a stone.

3. *A Resentment of Rabbits*

At our house not even the rabbits are scared.
    Why, they come out by day
and sit on the doorstep chewing euonymus leaves.
"Rabbit," we say to them, "Rabbit, go away.
    Feast on delicious weeds,
    alfalfa in the fields,
or dewberry blossoms under the night sky."
    Rabbit there on the step
    twitches a sensitive lip
and fixes us with the dot of a motionless eye.

4. *The Red Branch*

Sky after sky of windless blue;
warm days, but with a secret chill.
The forest wall is green except
for one red branch on the hill.

Quiet the leaves, as on a board
dead butterflies are pinned,
except for one red branch that stirs
in premonition of a wind.

Soon the September gale, too soon
the bare branch, the leaves blown.
Now, in the mid-September truce,
    one leaf drifts down.

5. *The Dog Fox*

When little daily winds have died away
and turkeys climb to roost in the apple tree,
across the snow night creeps so gradually
no eye can mark the cornerstone of day.

Now tightly draw the blinds against the dark
and see in lamplight how the room awakes.
Listen . . . through the tangible silence breaks,
out of the woodlot, a dog fox's bark.

A creak of rusty hinges in the wind:
his voice was like the rasping of a door,
and when it ceased the darkness instantly

became so hugely silent that behind
a final range of hills we heard the sea
grumbling with all his voices at the shore.

John Fenstermaker

All night waiting in an empty house,
under a dry electric moon that casts
no shadow, a man striding impatiently,
stroking the gray stubble on his cheek,
   sucking a cold pipe, waiting,
an empty sacrificial vessel waiting
without forbearance to be filled with God.

He says, "There was a scratching at the door,
the noise of someone fingering the latch,
once, but I opened and only found the night
empty of sound." The images of drought
possess his mind, acacias in the sand,
thorn-branched and thorny-leafed, that cast no shadow
by day, but quietly rustle in the night.

Beyond them rose a wall of enormous stones
laid without mortar, and a gateway barred
nightlong, lifelong. He pounded on the stones
and screamed. He pounds again on a closet door
in an empty house, then waits to hear the echo
come thundering back at him, mile after mile,
as walls crash down. This or some other night,

those gates will shatter open to the morning
and let him tread the morning streets of air.

Off Campus

"Your career and achievement"—
he skipped some words between dashes—
"are of abiding importance

to us and our reference users,"
and now the qualifying clause,
"although your sketch was transferred

some time ago to a non-current category
(because of retirement or other circumstances
affecting current national reference interest) ."

A printed card from *Who's Who*:
when the postman came sloshing through the snow
that morning, it was the only mail.

A radiator pounds in the living room
of the house he built with a whopping loan
the year they made him a full professor.

Water drips yellow from the bathroom faucet.
Paint flakes from the walls of his study.
The dust is white on his books.

"Please sign, date, and return card
even if no data additions are required."
Would there be any? he wondered.

His old wife putters in the kitchen;
now she is rinsing the breakfast dishes.
The pump comes on with a cardiac gasp.

"If biographee is no longer living,
recipient of card should kindly so
indicate on the space provided."

"I shall so indicate," he said—
the mortgage paid, his papers filed away,
his career and achievement filed away,

his heart filed away on a cardiogram,
his life on a punch card transferred
some time ago to a non-current category.

The Flower and the Leaf

All of an age, all heretics,
all rich in promise, but poor in rupees,
I knew them all at twenty-six,
when to a sound of scraping shovels,
emerging from whatever dream,
by night they left their separate hovels
as if with an exultant scream,
stamped off the snow and gathered round
a table at John Squarcialupi's,
happy as jaybirds, loud as puppies.

They were an omnicolored crew,
Midwesterner and Southerner,
New Yorker and New Englander,
immigrant, Brahman, Irish, Jew,
all innocent in their pride because
not one of them had grown a paunch
or lost faith in himself, or was
deformed by any strict belief.
I saw the flower and the leaf,
the fruit, or none, and the bare branch.

This man strains forward in his chair
to argue for his principles,
then stops to wipe his spectacles,
blink like a daylight owl, and shake
his janitor's mop of blue-black hair.
He can outquibble and outcavil,
laugh at himself, then speak once more
with wild illogic for the sake
of logic pure and medieval;

but all that night he will lie awake
to argue with his personal devil.

This man is studiously polite.
Good manners are an armor which
preserves for him an inner hush,
also, I think, a harbor light
that steers young ladies to his bed.
There was no hush that winter night
when flown with Squarcialupi's wine,
he made a funnel, then adopted
the look of a greedy child and said
in a five-beat iambic line,
having flung back his enormous head,
"All contributions gratefully accepted."

And this man, who has spent his day
wrestling with words, to make them mean
impossibly more than words convey,
now pours them out like a machine
for coining metaphors. He stalks
between the tables. His brown eyes
gleam like a leopard's as he talks
with effortless brilliance, then grow smaller
and veiled, the eyes of a caged fox.
Our money counted, dollar by dollar,
we taxi to Small's Paradise,
but Hart storms out to roam the docks
in search of some compliant sailor.

I think of the tangled reasons why
this man should flourish, this one die
obscurely of some minor hurt;
why this one sought his death by sea,
and this one drank himself to death,

and this one, not of our company,
but born on the same day as Hart,
should harvest all the world can give,
then put a gun between his teeth;
or why, among the friends who live,
this one misled by his good heart,
and this forsaken by a wench,
should each crawl off to nurse his grief.
I saw the flower and the leaf,
the fruit, or none, and the bare branch.

The famous and the forgotten dead,
the living, still without a wound,
I see them now at a sudden glance,
the possibly great, the grandly failed,
the doomed to modest eminence,
gathered once more, but not around
that table stained with dago red.
For some inconsequential reason,
I see them now in a hilltop field
on the first day of hunting season
and wonder if, on such a day
of misty, mild October weather,
they would be friend and equal still.
A sound of guns drifts up the hill,
a wind drives off the mist, and they,
brothers again, break bread together,
empty a pocket flask together.

The Urn

Wanderers outside the gates, in hollow
landscapes without memory, we carry
each of us an urn of native soil,
of not impalpable dust a double handful,

why kept, how gathered?—was it garden mould
or wood soil fresh with hemlock needles, pine,
and princess pine, this little earth we bore
in secret, blindly, over the frontier?

—a parcel of the soil not wide enough
or firm enough to build a dwelling on
or deep enough to dig a grave, but cool
and sweet enough to sink the nostrils in
and find the smell of home, or in the ears
rumors of home like oceans in a shell.

Index

Index of Titles and First Lines

A beauty it has that pleases some, 66
A man there is of fire and straw, 130
Allagazam, 71
All of an age, all heretics, 139
Always I felt a love for sordid things, 33
Angelica, 55
At our house not even the rabbits are scared, 134
At seven o'clock, when tables had been cleared, 6
August. On the vine eight melons sleeping, 110
Beach at Palavas, The, 60
Between the waves, out of the sight of land, 128
Beware of snogs, 117
Blown Door, The, 25
Blue Juniata, 5
Born in a fence corner, 81
Boy in Sunlight, 3
Buy 300 Steel, 74
Buy 300 steel at the, 74
Can you see their angular shadows on the blind, 40
Carnaval in the Midi, 63
Château de Soupir: 1917, 57
Chestnut Woods, The, 26
Circus in Town, 71
Commemorative Bronze, 84
Condemned to a red-plush room, 59
Dan George, 7
Day Coach, 21
Death is an accumulation of infirmities: hairs fall, 43
Dipping an adroit hand into his hat, he found, 75
Dog Fox, The, 135
Dry Season, The, 90

Dumbwaiter Song, 72
Eater of Darkness, The, 75
Eight Melons, 110
End of the World, The, 111
Enemy Within, The, 117
Ernest, 96
Every man his own Robespierre, 84
Ezra Pound at the Hôtel Jacob, 59
Farmhouses curl like horns of plenty, hide, 5
Firstborn, The, 92
Flower and the Leaf, The, 139
Flower in the Sea, The, 76
Following the dollar, ah, following the dollar, 49
For St. Bartholomew's Eve, 103
Free Clinic, 41
Fresh from the factory, 68
From the vast of it, 133
He chews tobacco, tips the dusty brim, 7
Here in a mountain valley, 12
Here on the table, a great scarred loaf of bread, 61
Here with the Long Grass Rippling, 119
Hill above the Mine, The, 10
I climbed the mountain, to its inmost crags, 90
I found a seed and planted it, 77
I met her in Chicago and she was married, 72
I saw them, yes, I saw their unbreathing armies, 105
I watched for years a sidehill farm that died, 25
I woke and could not see the familiar white, 100
I wonder—lying in the long grass, 119
In our country the barns are built four-square, 15
In the High Street of Cologne, 54
In the hot afternoon, 131
It was a noon of freedom, 91
Jean tells me that the Senator, 57
Jesus I saw, crossing Times Square, 76

—*jumped over the quick brown fox,* 116
Kelly's Barroom, 33
Knishes, kisses, 83
Lady from Harlem, The, 82
Last International, The, 105
Laurel Mountain, 13
Leander, 128
Leonora, I have rented an apartment, 72
Linda the manicurist, close beside, 36
Listen: we were working in the woods, 13
Living Water, The, 131
Long Voyage, The, 93
Lost People, The, 98
Love is the flower of a day, 34
Man of Promise, The, 94
Marizibill, 54
Memphis Johnny, 79
Mine No. 6, 9
Mortality, 43
Mother, The, 91
Mother has washed the dishes, limped upstairs, 37
Narrow House, The, 77
Natural History, 133
Nobody comes to the graveyard on the hill, 10
Nocturne, 37
Not that the pines were darker there, 93
Not the harsh voice in the microphone, 111
Nothing lives here, he says in the darkening room, 44
O masked ladies, excited with your dancing, 63
O sun of sleepless midnight, solitude, 112
Ode in a Time of Crisis, 116
Off Campus, 137
One morning during Carnaval they found two swans in the, 65
Out of an empty sky the dust of hours, 85
Overbeck's Barn, 15

Passport Blues, 114
Peppermint Gardens, The, 66
Piney Woods, 133
Poverty Hollow, 12
Processional of the Third Season, 19
Pyre, The, 27
Red Branch, The, 134
Resentment of Rabbits, A, 134
Restaurateur with Music, 83
Rocking Chairs, The, 6
Rows of soiled faces parallel, 41
Roxane, 97
Rubber Plant, The, 40
Safe is the man with blunderbuss, 96
Seven, 100
Silvery Fishes, The, 133
Sky after sky of windless blue, 134
Smoke of Birds, A, 62
So Perish Time, 44
Starlings descend at nightfall, wheeling, 62
Still Life, 61
Stone Horse Shoals, 125
Strangers were buying the house, 27
Sunrise over the Heiterwand, 51
Tar Babies, 95
Teeth on the saw, 133
Ten Good Farms, 86
Tennessee Blues, 72
The bedroom on the courtyard and the tree, 98
The boy having fished alone, 3
The fetish woman crossed the stage, 82
The house was full of light, 51
The well-bred children, the well-clipped grass, 94
The year declines now formally to his end, 19
The year swings over slowly, like a pilot, 78

Then die, 103
There Is a Moment, 127
There is a moment after the embrace, 127
They carry him off in a one-horse hack, 79
They scoured the hill with steel and living brooms, 9
This Morning Robins, 89
Tickets please tickets, 21
Those of Lucifer, 85
Three Songs for Leonora, 71
Time of Crossword Puzzles, The, 112
To wade the sea-mist, then to wade the sea, 125
Tomorrow Morning, 108
Tomorrow, walking in the dew-bright fields, 108
Translucent fingers on the yellow keys, 55
Tumbling Mustard, 81
Turning of the Year, The, 78
Two Swans, 65
Under a multitude of suns, 60
Urn, The, 142
Valuta, 49
Variations on a Cosmical Air, 34
Voices from Home: 1923, 68
Wanderers outside the gates, in hollow, 142
. . . was Flatbush born, was twenty-six, 97
What can I offer you now, now, 92
When everything but love was spent, 46
When I was a virgin, 114
When little daily winds have died away, 135
While nobody's million eyes are blinking, come, 26
William Wilson, 130
Winter Tenement, 46
With storm-washed gullies marking where the streets, 86
Yesterday snow, piled high on the black branches, 89
Young Mr. Androgyne, the talented poet, 95
Young Kuppenheimer Gods, 36
"Your career and achievement", 137